Bets & Breakfasts

A novella

Steven Cain

Two couples book a Murder & Mystery-themed cabin next to a casino for two weeks. The wives passionately enjoy the thrill of the haunted-looking house. None of the four anticipated the murder and mystery that waited for them below.

What people are saying!

Professor Michael J. Gaffney
Pullman, Washington

This suspense/horror story is a page-turner from the beginning. Steven Cain stretches his considerable writing talents into what is, for him, a new genre. With interesting characters and plot twists, this effort is a nice addition to Cain's authorship.

Leah Lederman
Indianapolis, Indiana

The characters and friendships in this book are as complicated as the halls of the eponymous Bets and Breakfasts Casino! Steven Cain navigates us through all of it, leading us to an unexpected end that will stay with us and leave us thinking about unintended consequences. This fun, campy thriller puts the creep in creepy.

Carla Johnson
Lafayette, Indiana

Bets and Breakfasts really captured my attention, and kept it. The way the story is told and the way the pertinent information is injected with such perfect timing is seamless! This book has the perfect ending.

**

What people say about Cain's other books!

War at Home

Lori Lehe – Round Grove, Indiana

Love and Lust. Fame and Fortune. Regrets and Retaliation. *War at Home* offers a fast-paced, thoughtful story of unquenchable desire. The desire ultimately asks: What are you willing to lose to win? Cain's storytelling is superb!

The Accident in Larson

Virginia Morgan White – Opelika, Alabama

What happens when you mix beautiful rural Indiana with a twenty-something smart guy, a sweetheart, and a mysterious car wreck? "The Accident in Larson" is an excellent story complicated by local and extraterrestrial forces. I loved the tw sts and turns. Thanks for an entertaining read.

Sunset Kings

Jane Ade Stevens – Indianapolis, Indiana

Sunset Kings is an unexpected story about the Hoffman farm family who experience the impact war can have for generations. From the cornfields of Belton County and the Blind Pig in Indianapolis to the magnificent French Jardin Botanique of Bailleu, Sunset Kings brings to life a story we rarely read about life on the farm.

Books by Steven Cain

Bets and Breakfasts - © 2023

Upon The Moment Publishing, LLC

Library of Congress Control Number: 2023901108

ISBN: 979-8-9863629-4-6

Sunset Kings © 2020 Upon the Moment Publishing, LLC

Library of Congress Control Number: 2021905234

ISBN: 978-1-7368362-0-0

The Accident in Larson © 2021 Upon the Moment Publishing, LLC

Library of Congress Control Number: 2021923613

ISBN: 978-1-7368362-4-8

War at Home – © 2022

Upon The Moment Publishing, LLC

Library of Congress Control Number: 2022904799

ISBN: 978-1-7368362-8-6

More Information at

https://www.stevenacain.com/

UPON THE
MOMENT
PUBLISHING

If you enjoy this novel, please tell a friend.

To
Kathryn 'Katt' Cain,
Because every day we write together
is precisely what we always hoped for us.

Kathryn 'Katt' Cain, who helped every step of the way.
Stephanie Cain for design creation and consulting.
Grammarly.com
Wikipedia

To My Readers

In 2022, I challenged myself to write a horror novella. You will find the results of that challenge on the following pages. I've told others that my first three novels were more like Hallmark. This novella is more like Hellmark. From others who have read the draft, this provided some scary moments. I hope you find it thrilling.

Second, I want to thank my daughter Stephanie Cain, who designed this cover and the covers for my three previous books. I bring this up because this cover represents the perfect match between human intelligence and talent and artificial intelligence. She read my description of the Murder & Mystery cottage mentioned in this book into an AI program and came up with this cover. Of course, she massaged the image AI created to perfect the cover. In all my years as a journalist and writer, I never guessed I'd write a book with a cover that brought out the best of both worlds.

Prologue Germany 1963

A woman screamed in pain. She fought fear while in labor in the backseat of a Volkswagen. Her husband attempted, in futility, to help her prepare for birth. They had stopped at a German carpark where another couple had instructed them to go.

The woman screamed again. Standing outside the car, the husband smelled smoke as if someone had burnt leaves nearby. He shook off the strange sensation and focused on the current situation.

The woman gave birth.

He looked at her with a face of apology and whispered, "Das baby ist Geboren. Es ist zwei!"

They had prepared for this moment. He donned plastic gloves. Years of driving an ambulance gave him the experience he needed. Deftly, he severed the umbilical cord from the mother in a sanitary fashion. He wanted to do what he had done many times in his ambulance deliveries and put the placenta above the baby until they reached a hospital. That practice would supply much-needed oxygen to the baby until it started breathing on its own. But he didn't know if the new parents could aseptically cut it away. He waited three minutes to ensure breathing began, then severed the cord to the placenta.

Carefully, he wrapped the bundle into a blanket, scanned the roadside area, and put the bundle on a picnic table as instructed. The smell of the smoke grew more robust. The man looked up and saw a dark cloud of smoke overhead. Trying to ignore it, he returned to the car and sat in the driver's seat. The woman painfully moved to the front passenger seat next to her husband. She winced when she sat and said, "Lassi tuns Diesen bösen Ort verlassen."

The husband nodded as he shifted the car into first gear and said, "Wir sind verdammt!" When he drove away, he looked into the rearview mirror and saw a grotesque-looking couple come out of the wooded area behind the carpark.

Two days ago, when they settled on a payment for the baby that the couple carried, the buyers had requested no one look at them. They hand-delivered the cash to the couple, rang the doorbell, and dashed. The husband never dreamed he would see them in the mirror. Both had long scraggly hair. They were shabbily dressed in dirty clothing and were missing teeth. The dwarf couple would never look like the natural parents, who were very tall. As he drove away, the husband wiped tears from his eyes as if it wiped away their sins of cruelty. The odd-looking couple had paid 10,000 Deutsche Mark for a baby. They found a bonus wrapped in the towel.

Chapter 1 Indiana July 29, 1998

Two men and two women wandered around a bodega looking for snacks and last-minute supplies. They chatted aimlessly among themselves while shopping. "How far are we from the place?" asked Tom Martin. He stood a head taller than everyone in the bodega. Tall and skinny, his face stood out with two days of stubble. His right hand stood out also as he reached for a bag of chips. His ring and pinky fingers contracted back upon themselves, a condition of Dupuytren contracture. Tom often bragged about it, saying, "It's a Viking disease. It proves I have Viking blood in me."

Olivia, Tom's wife, chimed in, "The Bets and Breakfasts resort is just around the corner. So, let's get what we need and get going," She dangled the car keys in the air. While not as tall as Tom, she stood 5' 11". Not skinny, her stocky frame made her a perfect college basketball player, where Tom, as an assistant coach, met her for the first time.

Unbeknownst to the two couples, a man called Jeck watched them move about the bodega. His facial expression tensed when he heard their destination was the Bets and Breakfasts, the most modern Bed and Breakfast motif in Indiana, maybe even the nation. He hoped it would be the "Murder & Mystery" themed guest house.

Andre looked at Destiny and said, "Don't forget the ice."

Destiny, who inspected a different soap for black skin than she had seen before, said, "Oh like that's the wife's job to get the ice." She grabbed the soap, and despite her protest, the beautiful young woman turned toward the ice kiosk and immediately bumped into the stranger who had watched them, especially her, since they entered the store. Her sunglasses slipped down her face, so she pushed them back upon her nose. The muscular stranger stood his ground, and she shook in shock because she felt he was sexually aroused when she accidentally pressed into him. Not wanting to think about that or acknowledge his aroused state, she quickly backed away while looking at the floor. Not seeing the man's face, she said, "Excuse me."

The man silently stood his ground.

She walked back to Andre and whispered, "You go get the ice. That man scares me."

Andre scoped the man as he moved past him to the ice machine. The man didn't look at him but kept intensely eyeing

Destiny. Andre said, "Watch it, pig. That's my wife, you startled." With that comment, the man turned and looked at him for the first time. He stood five inches taller than Andre and outweighed him by fifty pounds. Jeck's round face and cold-eyed stare sent shivers down Andre's back. Sternly, Andre said, "Just mind your own business, creep!" Then, oddly, Andre noticed the man had an unusual scent. As he moved to the ice kiosk, he thought about baseball when they used lime to mark the field. This man smelled like that. Andre grabbed a bag of ice, returned to Destiny, and whispered, "I can see why he creeped you out."

Jeck didn't utter a word while the couples checked out at the cash register. He slid behind them, hurried out the door, and proceeded to the Bets and Breakfasts. The stranger didn't exit completely unnoticed. The cashier shook her head and looked at Destiny. "You're not alone, dear. That guy creeps me out every time he comes in here."

Olivia attempted an evil laugh when the foursome hopped back into the Dodge Charger. With witch-like hands held above the steering wheel, she said, "Maybe he comes with the Murder & Mystery cottage that we rented for the next two weeks."

Sitting in the back seat, Destiny grabbed Andre's hand, squeezed it, and said, "That's not the way I want to be frightened at our rental."

Andre asked, "Did you see how he stared at you?"

"I didn't see his face at all."

Olivia looked at Destiny in the rearview mirror and said, "He was very plain looking. He looked a little older than us. His face was fat, and he had a shaved head."

Andre chimed in, "But what stood out the most was his coal-black eyes on that ashen face."

Destiny mumbled, "That wasn't what stood out the most!"

Tom said, "Forget him. Let's get to the Bets and Breakfasts so we can unpack and go gambling."

Chapter 2

Moments later, Olivia drove the car slowly into the driveway of the Murder & Mystery-themed cottage. She and her three passengers stared at the large, dark, evil-looking rental.

"Looks as though we got our money's worth," Andre said while pushing the window release button to open it. When he stuck his head out, he gaped at the house. "That's scarier than shit."

Destiny thought about saying, *You didn't pay a dime of the two-week rent, Andre.* Instead, she said, "I told you it would be. It's the Murder & Mystery-themed Bets and Breakfasts that I booked on the internet. I think it is deliciously evil-looking. It's the only rental of its kind. We are lucky we got it. I must say that I love our new internet."

Olivia continued driving the car slowly up the winding driveway bordered by tall, black rocks that hid the car from view from the road. "Dee, you certainly have outdone yourself this time, girl. This looks perfect to help us celebrate my birthday tomorrow."

Tom added, "You are one twisted sister, but I love that."

The house featured three gabled roofs with spires on each one. A large white clock with black hands that permanently pointed at the 12 adorned the middle-gabled roof that rose above the two shorter ones. Andre said, "Hey, look, it appears the clock is on permanent midnight!" He assumed correctly. Four large windows with equally black shutters with spire-like shapes pointed up and down over the house's dark, grey stone surface. Black wrought iron bars crisscrossed each of the four windows.

Pleased with herself, Destiny sported a huge smile and said, "I can't wait to see inside."

Tom exclaimed, "I can't wait to walk to the casino and start winning at the slot machines."

Behind the house stood a thick briarwood that hid Jeck, the tall, chubby man Destiny had bumped into at the bodega. He knew how to hide in the briarwood and yet closely observe the foursome. He watched the two couples walk around the outside of the house. At the back door, they entered a code to open it. Jeck waited until they disappeared into the house before he stepped out of the woods and up to the back of a shack behind the creepy house. With his key, he opened the pitch-black door, stepped into the shack, and immediately proceeded down a set of stairs to a tunnel that led into the hidden basement of the foursome's rental house. Jeck had lived there for just under a year.

Tom jumped up and down and protested that the other three took too much time getting ready for the casino. "I want to go to the casino now!" He could have gone alone, but he didn't enjoy leaving Olivia behind, especially on their first visit to this casino.

Olivia said, "Hold your horses. We want to look as beautiful as possible in case we get a better offer tonight." She donned her special smile from which Tom would forgive her anything. He rolled his eyes and laughed.

An hour later, when the four entered the casino, they heard the usual jangly music, the whir of spinning reels, and loud beeps and chimes. They smelled heavy cigarette smoke wafting through the casino. For some, that smell was a relaxing invitation to imbibe in another smoke. For others, it was a cloying smell that their bodies rejected. None of the four smoked. Destiny's allergies to the smoke meant she would develop a headache, but she enjoyed gambling too much, so she put up with it. Oblivious to the smell, Tom rubbed his hands and felt at home. All four parted ways and found their type of vice. Tom hustled to the slot machines, Olivia to the blackjack table, Andre to the poker table, and Destiny walked up to the roulette wheel. Before she sat, in her typical fashion, she glanced around the room to see if anyone noticed her. Of course, two men stood at the bar observing her beauty and shared lewd comments among themselves about what they would do with her if either got her alone.

Two and a half hours later, which included high-energy, if not high-stakes gambling, and many alcoholic drinks, they headed back to the rental for the night. Andre, Olivia, and Destiny all bragged that they walked away with a little more money than they had started with that day. Tom followed them quietly and moaned at their bragging.

"What's up with you, Tom?" Andre asked.

"I don't want to say."

"Oh, come on, it can't be that bad. How much did you lose?"

"One-hundred and fifty."

"On the slot machines?"

"Hey, I was busy and sure thought my luck would change at some point."

Andre patted him on the back as they walked and said, "Maybe better luck tomorrow. Did you bring enough money?"

Tom looked him in the eye and said, "Twenty times that amount. I'm a high roller."

Under the house, in the secret rooms, Jeck hid from the drunken couples who noisily clambered into the kitchen. They stuffed snacks into their faces and laughed about it. Olivia snickered as she munched down on a giant, soft, doughy pretzel. "This is just what I needed after all those martinis," she said loudly.

Jeck stood in the dark room below the kitchen. The video and audio feed from hidden cameras and microphones on the main floor projected onto a large screen and equally large speakers. He listened and watched them. It made him feel as if he stood among them. "They are noisier than the last group, and the two women are gorgeous."

"Be quiet. Those people may hear you."

"You be quiet. I can't hear when you talk."

Jeck cupped a hand to his ear. "I think they are going to bed now."

"I need to hurry then." He stepped into the next room, where a ladder allowed him to climb up a vertical, hidden shaft to Andre's and Destiny's bedroom. Silently, he opened a secret door and slid under the high-posted bed where the couple would sleep. He waited for them to come to bed.

Eventually, Andre and Destiny stumbled into the bedroom as they pulled their clothes off and climbed together onto the bed. Destiny smoothed her hands over the black satin duvet. "This is nice. Let's make love on it!"

Andre looked under the bed and said, "It's strange how tall this bed is. It's sitting on an ornate box." He saw evil faces painted on the solid wood border under the bed. He laughed and added, "Maybe someone is hiding under there. Maybe it's that hyena from the bodega."

Destiny smacked his muscular shoulder. "That's too creepy. Don't change my mood for sex. You creep." It didn't change her mind; minutes later, they romped on the bed.

The stranger under the bed smiled and lightly touched the underside of the box springs as the couple began moving up and down rhythmically. He closed his eyes and slowly brought his hands to his chest as he lay on the false floor in the box under their bed. He felt their motion through the movement of the bed springs. When Andre moaned loudly, the supine man moved his right hand down to his erect penis and stroked it.

Andre said, "That's it, baby. You know I like it when you squeeze me like that. I-I can't hold back anymore! Aagh...ugh!"

Under the bed, the man orgasmed quietly without a peep or a moan. He lay silently and listened to the couple as they cuddled and whispered to each other, but that ended quickly when Andre began to snore. Destiny smirked quietly, "Snore away, honey. I'll take care of myself like I usually do."

As Andre snored, the man under the bed heard Destiny moan while squeaking the bedsprings. Destiny's actions were an encore performance he would never forget.

Chapter 3 July 30

The next morning, Olivia walked into the kitchen, where Tom and Destiny chorused, "Surprise!" They sang, "Happy Birthday to you! Happy Birthday to You!" They continued the song and pushed a cake with lit candles toward Olivia's end of the table.

Olivia curtsied and lightly placed a finger on her red cheek. She bent to blowout the candles on the cake and said, "I'm glad you didn't try to match the number of years." Tom slid a small package across the table toward Olivia. "What's this?"

"You have to open it to see."

She opened it carefully and exposed a jewelry box. She walked over to Tom and sat on his lap while she opened the box. She gasped and smiled when she saw the ring inside. It was a dolphin ring with two green emeralds for eyes and a not-so-tiny diamond on its nose. It resembled the dolphin playing with a beachball. She turned and kissed Tom on each cheek and then landed a big kiss on his mouth. Destiny looked at the beautiful ring and wished that Andre would treat her with something like that. She said, "Well, girl, go on. Put it on." She admired Tom and Olivia's relationship, even though she fought a little jealousy. 'Shame on me,' she said to herself. At the appropriate time, she handed Olivia her gift.

"Pour Moi?" Olivia asked with one hand toward her chest.

"Yes, but you don't need to sit on my lap!"

"Oh, what's the fun in that?" She leaped up, scuttled toward Destiny, and sat on her lap. Destiny feigned that Olivia crushed her. Olivia opened the gift and pulled out a cameo neckless of mother-of-pearl. Instead of a human face, it sported two dolphins kissing. "Awe, you guys went together on this. How cool!"

Olivia started to kiss Destiny, but the latter laughed and said, "Not going there, girl."

Tom volunteered, "I'll watch!"

Both women looked at him sternly and chorused, "Perv!"

All three laughed.

Andre walked into the kitchen and asked, "Where's breakfast? We are staying in a Bets and Breakfasts place, right?"

Olivia stood, looked at him, standing in his t-shirt and boxers, and said, "Why don't you clean up and get dressed? Then we will all go over to the casino, where we get our free

16

breakfasts." Andre had not realized the casino hosted the complimentary breakfasts.

Stepping up to her husband, Destiny frowned, turned him around, and started to push him to the stairs toward the bedroom. She stopped and turned Andre back around to look at Olivia. "Don't you have something to say to Olivia?"

"Oh, happy birthday." He puckered as if to kiss her.

"Not until you brush your teeth. You smell like a brewery."

Destiny turned Andre around and nudged him toward the stairs. "Git yourself ready to go, you git. We are all famished." Andre turned and sauntered up the stairs. The other three feasted on the birthday cake.

A half-hour later, the foursome loaded their plates at an all-you-can-eat breakfast buffet. Andre nudged Destiny with his elbow and said, "Be subtle but look over by the slot machines. That pig you ran into at the bodega yesterday is watching you?"

Destiny didn't look up while piling bacon on her plate. "I wouldn't know. I never looked at his face, and you are really creeping me out."

Andre continued, "He has turned away. Look now. I think he's wearing the same clothes that he had on yesterday."

She looked at his feet and said, "Yes, those are the same loafers he wore yesterday." She turned her attention back to the buffet. "What are the chances we'd see him two days in a row?"

"I think he's checking you out."

She shoved Andre with an elbow, "Get outta town. Your imagination runs too wild. It's just a coincidence."

The couple walked away from the buffet and sat next to Tom and Olivia. Andre said, "You haven't seen how he stares at you. It's as if I don't exist."

Tom spoke up, "You talkin' about the ghoulish guy over by the slot machines?"

Andre nodded.

"He was there last night. Standing at the end of that row of machines. I think he distracted me and caused my unlucky streak."

"The roulette wheel is on that side of the slot machines, Tom. I'll tell you, he wasn't checking on you. He scoped out Destiny."

Destiny put two fingers on Andre's lips, "Be quiet now. You are starting to become creepy yourself." She studied Andre to see how he would react to her admonishment.

He looked at her and saw the confident, beautiful eyes that he loved. Andre shrugged and said, "Okay. I'll be quiet, but I'll keep an eye on him. He…"

Destiny put her fingers back on his lips and intoned a firm, "Hush...." By singing the word 'hush with a sibilant sound, Andre knew she had become annoyed at his persistence. He sat silently and finished his breakfast.

Olivia changed the subject. "After some gambling, let's explore the cottage more. I found a treasure map on the entryway table. It's supposed to help us explore the place and learn more about the macabre that it displays."

Destiny chirped, "I like that idea."

The men rolled their eyes because they knew they were outnumbered ever if the vote was two to two.

After breakfast, they all placed some bets but agreed to return to the cottage earlier than usual at Destiny's insistence. The men slowly followed the eager treasure hunters out of the casino. Two young men approached the foursome just outside the casino door and away from security. The men walked alongside them with their backs turned toward security. One of the men reached into a pocket and produced some joints in a small Ziplock baggie. He didn't say a word but gave a look of, "Do you want some?"

Andre immediately gave him a look that said, 'Yes.' "How much?"

"The price depends on how much you want."

Andre looked at the baggie. He estimated four joints in it. "The whole baggie."

The stranger didn't hesitate. "Twenty bucks."

"That's pretty pricey for four joints."

"Hey, they are already rolled."

"Fifteen."

The stranger held out a hand while all six continued to walk. Andre pulled fifteen dollars out of his wallet. The two exchanged the money for the joints. At that, the second man pulled out a bag of coke. He said, "While we're talking, how about some of this."

Tom stopped walking and looked at the cocaine. Olivia's mouth dropped when she watched Tom stare at the cocaine. "Surely you are not falling back to that, especially on my birthday."

She turned and walked away from Tom, folded her arms across themselves, and stood with a look of disgust. Tom hadn't seen cocaine in a few years, and the addiction immediately thrust him back to those years. He yearned for the drug with a force that swept to his brain. He looked at the other man and then at Olivia, who didn't return the look. Shaking a bit, he put a hand up toward the second man and cleared his throat. "N-no, thank you," he said. With those words, he conquered the addiction. He didn't conquer the feeling of abandonment he felt from Olivia.

The second man shrugged and said, "Well, it's your loss." The two men walked away.

Olivia turned back to Tom with tears in her eyes and said, "Thank you, babe." She choked back an almost verbal cry.

"Anything for you!" He fought back the feeling of abandonment and walked up to her and took her hand.

They all walked silently, reflecting on what happened, wins and losses during the morning gambling, and even how they felt about each other. They followed a trail through the woods between the casino and their cottage. Sunlight broke through the woods as the four walked in and out of sunbeams and shade. The shade helped cool them in the hot Indiana weather. More importantly, the woody fragrance provided a mild transition from the smokey casino to the cottage.

When they approached it, they each gazed at the Murder & Mystery rental. Destiny, tickled with herself for finding the place, smiled and silently acknowledged her accomplishment. Andre wondered how much it cost, but he wouldn't find out because she would never reveal the cost to him. She knew he couldn't afford it. Oddly enough, or in Andre's way, he never asked her. Olivia wondered why they hadn't explored it more last night, but in a moment of realization, she looked at Tom and remembered that he hurried them out of the cottage last night to go gambling. She thought *I'll take a gambling addition over a drug addiction any day. At least he knows how to control the gambling.*

Inside, Destiny unfolded the Murder & Mystery map and pointed to the grandfather clock just inside the front door. She read the description, "It says here that the howls are that of a Eurasian wolf found in Norway."

"That howl kept me up half the night," Andre said.

Destiny wanted to say, 'You snored most of the night.' She refrained.

Andre added, "Our bedroom is closest to the clock. I'm silencing it." He walked toward the clock and looked for a door in the back.

Destiny shouted, "Wait! Wait! It says this is a replica of the grandfather clock that Sir Wendell Warding of Denmark invented. It goes on to say that he hated squatting relatives at his castle so much, he paid to have it howl every hour." She glanced at the clock. "Hey, it's three 'till the hour. Now that we know its purpose, let's listen one more time before we disable it."

Andre moaned, but he complied.

Tom saw a beautifully embroidered rope hanging from the ceiling next to the clock. To Olivia's scolding, he pulled on it. Nothing happened. "It's just a rope."

Still standing near the grandfather clock, Destiny said, "It's not just a rope. It resembles the rope that Sir Warding used to hang himself when relatives wouldn't leave. He could no longer stand them and listen to the clock howling."

"Payback is a bitch," Andre said with a new respect for the rope.

Even though they stood looking at the clock for another minute, they all jumped when the loud howling sound emanated from the clock. After the howling stopped, three of them chuckled, but Andre repositioned the clock, opened the back door, and disabled the device.

"There! Why didn't Sir Warding do that instead of hanging himself."

Olivia suggested, "It probably had more to do with the insufferable, squatting relatives."

Tom nodded, but even though he wouldn't admit it to the others, he became very curious about the objects in the rental cabin. Ready to move on, he approached a door. Like many doors in the cottage, the knob was a shrunken, fake skull like the ones he had read about in pigmy stories. "Hey, we haven't gone into this room. Let's find out what's in here," he tugged at the door.

but it wouldn't open. Frustrated, he tugged on it a couple more times. It didn't budge.

"What's the matter, big boy? Can't you open it," Olivia teased as she sauntered up to the door. "Let me try." She felt a click when she touched the knob. After the click, she opened the door with ease. She looked at the astonished others and said, "Tom must have jarred it loose."

They couldn't have known what really happened. Jeck watched them from a monitor in the basement. When Olivia touched the door, he pushed a button to release the door.

They wrote it off to Olivia's words that Tom must have jarred it because they all stood dumbfounded at what they saw. A wall with no passage stood behind the door and frame. "That's an ugly wall," Olivia said. "It doesn't match the beautiful wood on the wall around the door." They saw white wallpaper with four dirty handprints and a stylized, large, outlined eye in blue. It appeared to be hand drawn. What might have been considered beautiful, the eye chilled all four of them!

It was Destiny who understood its meaning. "It's an evil eye. This is from ancient Persia. They even have amulets today with eyes shaped like this." Then she frowned and glanced at the map. She pointed out where they stood. "Huh, the funny thing is this door and eye are not on the map."

Olivia said, "It's like it's intended to scare us away."

"That's what it's supposed to do."

"It's doing a great job of that," Andre said.

Another chilling aspect involved the Omni view of the eye. Each thought that the unblinking eye stared at them as if they were all locked into its gaze. "That's weird," Tom said as he felt the wallpaper all the way to the door frame edges. "This is not a door, but a frame for this evil-eye-design on the wall." He gently took the outer doorknob from Olivia and closed it back onto the wall. That time they all heard the door click into place against the wall. "I think we will leave that alone."

"It made the hair on the back of my neck stand up," Andre said. "Let's forget about it."

Destiny didn't know if she could forget the eye behind the door to nowhere, but bravely she said, "Let's move on."

They walked into the next room and looked at a painting on the wall. They had seen it the night before, but they didn't look at it until the moment they re-entered that room. They saw a dark wooden sofa with wood armrests curved up and away on each side. The seat and back featured thick cushions with wild paisley teardrop designs. Instead of adding richness to the couch, it made them all feel as if the couch cried. Above the sofa, a large, heavy, framed oil painting hung, depicting an autopsy.

The cadaver lay on the table in the painting and stared a dead blank stare toward the sky. The corpse's skin glowed white as if it had been dusted with powdered lime. The examiner who peered over the cadaver appeared larger than life. For some unknown reason, the painter made him huge. Destiny thought his smile was too broad, making him look like he enjoyed splitting the dead person open. But what stood out the most to Olivia and Tom was the color of the paint that represented the blood. Again, Tom could not resist. He reached out and touched the paint that literally appeared to drip from the painting. He felt a little spark as he touched it, so he pulled his hand back quickly. He thought it through and decided to touch it again. This time there was no spark, so he wrote it off to static electricity or being afraid to touch the picture the first time. He slowly shook his head, "This place is starting to get to me."

"I warned you about this place. Isn't it great?" Destiny asked and laughed a fake evil laugh. She read from the map. "This painting depicts a mass killer in Boston who, when he ran out of bodies, began to dissect his own. His name was Dr. Max Brentarm. He died in 1833. Police officials found him days after his death with his intestines splayed out of his body, draping toward the floor. The sofa replicates the one he sat on when he watched his victims die."

Tom said, "Let's go back into the dining room. I want to hear what the map says about it."

As they entered the room - where they had sat for dinner the night before - it looked completely different because of their heightened mood. Andre had assumed everything was make-believe, like a haunted house, and had no connection with reality. Olivia had no clue that everything was recreated from bizarre real-life incidents. That said, the dining room became the pièce de rèsistance. It mace the house complete. With the help of the map, Destiny explained that the dining room featured medieval torture-chamber artifacts, including a table with knives carved into the wood. Gears and chains adorned the two ends of the table and gave it the look of a rack. Heretic's forks stood in a cabinet. Olivia explained that monks employed them during the Spanish Inquisition. With dual prongs placed at both ends, monks forced them between the breastplate and chin of the person they tortured during the Inquisition. The victim could not talk or sleep, which drove them into delirium. Destiny knew the meaning of "me retracto" engraved into the forks. "Yeh, I learned it a long time ago. It means 'I recant.' She felt disgusted that they used these forks for dining last night.

They talked about the cold chills they felt as they learned more about the cabin. Last night, they had rushed to check in and get on with the business of gambling. Tonight, they sat around the dining table/torture table and told scary stories to add to the treat. That was the nature of this group.

Returning to their bedrooms, each couple looked more closely at the adornments. Both rooms featured tall four-post beds. Andre and Destiny's bed featured serpentine posts made of a green, hydrated magnesium silicate compressed to give a realistic snake-skin appearance. At the top of the serpent posts, giant snakeheads curved away from the bed as if they guarded those who slept there. Carved wooden elephants with white tusks stood on smashed snakes and served as bedside tables. The wall above the headboard in Andre and Destiny's room looked like a large tunnel with an eerie light glowing from around a curve in the tunnel. It gave Andre the jitters as if something lurked around the corner. "Okay. Okay. This place has officially gotten to me," he said.

Destiny padded him on a shoulder and said, "Settle down, big guy. It's all just fantasy. It will be a great show for us in the next two weeks."

Andre looked at his wristwatch and saw that it was 11:11 p.m. He huffed on the watch and buffed it with a cleaning cloth that he kept next to the bed. Andre had a wristwatch fetish. His collection included ten very expensive watches and one very inexpensive watch, of which he brought three on this trip. To settle himself, he pulled them out of his suitcase along with supplies and began cleaning them. This distraction didn't bother Destiny, who had learned how important the watches were to Andre. She shuffled to the bathroom and began to polish herself.

The watches varied with his attitude the day he bought them. Over the years, he had visited several collectible's stores. Each of his watches had jumped out at him when he found them in various stores.

His first purchased watch set him back $400 when he found it in a curio shop in upstate New York. He had gone to the New York burg as a guest lecturer at a small college. Of course, he had to check out the local curio shop a colleague had recommended. One watch stood out because it appeared to be see-through at first. On closer inspection, he saw the rotating parts consisted of bone. He asked and found that the bone came from road-kill animals. That intrigued Andre that someone would commit the time to clean roadkill, shave off bone chips, and put them into a wristwatch. Cleaning the watch, Andre felt the same excitement as he did the day he found it. At the Murder & Mystery cabin, he sat and polished it while Destiny stood in front of the bathroom mirror admiring her good fortune in her beauty.

The second watch came from a student with whom he had sex. She seduced him rather than the other way around, but he didn't resist. After a night of romping, the student sat up to leave and put her watch back on. That caused Andre to notice it.

"Oh my god, that's a rare watch! Where did you get it?" The student sat quietly, not wanting to tell him how she got it. He pressed on. "What made you buy that watch?"

She slightly shook her head side-to-side. She pursed her lips and admitted, "I didn't buy it. If you must know, an ex-boyfriend gave it to me."

"Wow, he must have loved you very much or had a lot of money."

"In his way, he loved me, but he wanted to possess me, and that's not what I wanted."

"I want that watch!"

She took it off her wrist, ready to give it to him, but then said, "How much?"

Andre would have paid $500 for it or stolen it from her the next time they slept together, but he read the student well. "I'll offer $200."

Being a student from a low-income family, that was a lot of money. Her eyes widened, but then she halted. "Do you have that much money on you?"

Andre reached for his wallet, opened it, and pulled out $200. He handed it to her without saying it left him with a measly $12 for the rest of the month. She grabbed the money and tossed the watch at him. Even though they were sitting on the bed, Andre reached out with both hands and caught it as if it was a raw egg.

His parents had given him the third watch – which he brought on this trip - on his seventh birthday. The Timex watch had been with him most of his life. He always thought his seventh year was the best year of his life. Andre credited the watch for bringing him good luck. Not coincidently, it started his watch-collecting habits. He never thought his watch fetish might be the beginning of his demise.

The wall on one side of Tom and Olivia's room featured a painting of a spiderweb with a giant 3-D black spider appearing to crawl out of the corner of the ceiling. "It's creepy looking. I wonder why the casino chose a huge, real-looking spider." Tom said, "Some people wouldn't be able to put up with that."

Olivia said, "Definitely not Destiny. When she researched this place, she learned about the giant spider. That's why we have this room, and she didn't follow us here." She snickered about Destiny's issue with spiders as she walked to one of the large, barred windows which looked out into the night. She barely made out the view below the window. There appeared to be a small, icky shack between the house and the briarwood. Olivia said, "We need to check that out more tomorrow." Before she turned to go back to bed, she placed a hand on a miniature black gargoyle. There was one on each inside corner of the window. In turn, she gazed at all four of them. Instinctively, she bent forward to examine one more closely. Raising her voice, she said, "Hey Tom, come look at these gargoyles."

She had no idea what happened in the basement. The gargoyle that she looked at possessed a hidden microphone. Standing so close to the object with her raised voice, it blared from the speakers Jeck used to listen to them. Jeck jumped in a startle that he hadn't felt in a long time because her voice clamored in the basement. Recovering from the surprisingly loud voice, a smile grew on his face.

In the middle of the night, Jeck snuck out to the car. He enjoyed listening to them so much that he decided to bug Olivia's car. The task was easy. He mounted a wireless microphone under the front dash of Olivia's car. The procedure took only moments as he clipped it into place. He placed a remote camera where he could look up between their thighs. The camera cost him a fortune but only a tiny portion of his casino winnings. A few years back, Jeck had won the largest single-dollar bet on a slot machine at a different casino.

He couldn't use a battery to power the camera because the size would be prohibitive, so he rearranged a few fuses to power the camera when anyone started the car. His smile grew more when he completed the job. He rubbed his hands because he couldn't wait for Olivia to drive the car. He hoped she would wear a short skirt when she did. Quietly, he closed the car door and retreated to the basement.

Chapter 4 Friday, July 31

Olivia woke with a mild hangover. She patted Tom on the shoulder while he slept contently. She adored him when he slept as when he was awake. He gave her everything she ever wanted in a relationship, love, companionship, a sense of security, adventure, and a feeling that she was an equal. After looking him over for a minute, she turned and attempted to get out of bed. Her hangover headache caused her to sit down. She pressed a hand to her forehead as if to reload her mind for another day. Quietly she said to herself as she walked to the bathroom, "Just like that, another birthday has come and gone. Why do they go by so quickly now?"

Tom's response startled her, "I can tell you why."

"You were supposed to be asleep and not be listening. But go ahead with your reason why. I'm curious."

Tom got out of bed and scratched his private parts while he walked to the bathroom. Olivia looked into the mirror while Tom lifted the toilet seat and urinated.

Olivia thought *I'll take the good with the bad.*

Tom yawned. Olivia immediately thought of a monkey. Then he said, "Well when you first start to have a concept of time, let's say, five years old. A year is one-fifth of your life and all your experiences." He stopped urinating, put his penis back in his shorts, and flushed. "But at age 29, a year is only one-twenty-ninth of your life and your entire consciousness. That's why it seems shorter." He expanded his lips and looked at his teeth in the mirror.

Olivia burst out laughing. "So, the monkey spews Einstein." Then she thought to herself, *And a sense of humor.*

An hour later, the four visited the shack before walking to the casino for breakfast. They guessed the casino owners had painted the window black and locked the doors. Andre guessed it was a storage house designed to add to the spookiness of the property instead of looking like a suburban tool shack.

They had no clue Jeck used the shed to move from the briarwood into the tunnel to the hidden rooms under the house.

Gambling after breakfast paid off for Tom. In three hours, he garnered $364 at the slot machines. He lost about $80 because he picked up the four pitchers of blood orange mimosas they had drunk. Feeling light-hearted and lite headed, they retreated from the casino to their Murder & Mystery cottage.

Tom didn't hold back bragging as they walked back.

"Cool down, tiger!" Andre laughed as he rebuked Tom, "I'm not sure we need to hear all this just because you bought the drinks."

All four laughed. Olivia noted that the day had become very hot, and the walking didn't help them cool down. "Well, it is the end of July, and it is southern Indiana. The humidity is stifling."

"Maybe it's time we skinny-dip in the lake," Destiny shocked everyone with the suggestion, but Tom and Olivia shared their approval. Andre took a side-long glance at Destiny.

"I'm not sure I want my woman showing herself in public in the daylight," he hesitated.

Destiny's jaw dropped, and she mouthed 'my woman' and accentuated it with her arms in the air with imitated quotation marks with her fingers.

Andre continued, "I don't want my woman outdoors nude, especially in front of Tom." He glanced at the others, laughed, and said, "Just kidding." The foursome had skinny-dipped on previous getaways.

Within moments of removing their clothes in the bedrooms, the men ran down the hill to the lake, flung off their robes and flip flops, and jumped into the water. The women trailed behind several minutes later and were much more subdued. When they reached the water's edge, Olivia giggled slightly and tensed her neck and jaws because of nervousness. "Are we going to do this here in the daylight?" She looked at Destiny, who had already disrobed and stood on a boulder at the water's edge.

She posed like a Siren and sang, "The brierwood hides us from the others, and the cottages across the lake are so far away. So far away." She posed with one arm pointing toward the far side of the lake while Tom and Andre glared at her from the water.

Olivia, who thought Destiny was a bit vain, especially in front of Tom, said, "Oh, you are always so melodramatic when it comes to nudity." She then jumped off a rock into the lake and doused Destiny with the resulting splash of water.

Destiny tried to fend off the splash with her arms and hands, but she still posed for the trio. "Help me. Help me. I'm melting!" She drew her hands to her face in an obvious attempt to imitate the famous wicked witch. She laughed and finally jumped into the lake.

Hiding in the briarwood, Jeck rubbed himself through his trousers. *They are so much better than past guests at this cottage. I wish I could keep Destiny here for the rest of her life.*

He had sat behind a tree and peered around it at the two women while they entered the lake and floated on their backs. Quietly he watched and orgasmed while the foursome played in the water.

With the sun setting on the lake, Andre stoked a bonfire between the lake and the cottage.

Destiny said matter-of-factly, "He's a pyro, and this is his heaven."

Soon they all took in the scent of burning cedar. Andre enjoyed the glowing embers growing below the pile of burning wood. Olivia immediately hungered for food from the scent of the fire, and Destiny longed for a romantic time with Andre and her friends.

While Andre attended the fire, Tom warmed up his acoustic guitar. Olivia said, "He's really very good, especially considering he had to switch hands because of the condition."

Tom grew up playing the guitar right-handed. Because of the early onset of Viking's disease on this right hand, which bent the two fingers inward toward the palm, he switched hands. Strumming the guitar, Tom noted, "I think it was Mark Knopfler who said a guitar is fickle. If you do this...," He stroked the guitar, which made a perfect tune, "you have to do this with the strings." He moved his fingers and continued, "But if you do this, you must rearrange your hand and fingers to do this." Again, the tune resounded in the wooded area, to everyone's delight. With the notes, Destiny knew what song came next.

As Tom played in earnest, Destiny sang.

Here comes Tommy singing oldies, goldies
"Be-bop-a-Lula, Baby, what I say."

Destiny pointed a long finger at Tom and winked. Olivia, who couldn't carry a tune in a wheelbarrow, felt a tinge of jealousy. She silently admonished herself for the thought. Clear and soothing to the ears, Destiny continued singing while Tom played. The sunset illuminated the lake, and the reflected light lit Destiny's face. She soaked up the spotlight.

He watched and listened to them play from a small window in the apex of the cottage. Destiny's singing became orgasmic for him, who had heard so few performances like hers.

Chapter 5 Saturday, August 1

Andre picked through the buffet carefully each morning. He suffered severely from food allergies. He questioned the chefs about how they prepared some items. Often frustrated, many cooks never understood that his allergies were life-threatening. The wrong oil for grilling, such as fish oil, could kill him within minutes. What made it worse was that lower and mid-class cooks thought if it said vegetable oil, it would be okay for people allergic to fish oil. They didn't understand that a simple switch in the type of vegetable oil could be just as deadly for Andre. Food companies list soybean and peanut oil as vegetable oil, but they could be fatal for Andre. He often told chefs that vegetable oils with canola or corn were fine. Among many other issues, he had celiac disease accentuated by an intense allergy that only 0.005 percent of the population experienced. The doctors diagnosed him perfectly, but unfortunately, they knew of no cure.

Summer 1993

Destiny and Andre had met at a clinic five years before. Both suffered from severe allergies but in different forms. Andre fought food allergies that could put him into anaphylactic shock and kill him. Destiny developed exercise-induced bronchoconstriction, often called EIB, due to severe dust and pollen allergies. While it is rarely fatal, it severely limited Destiny's participation in sports.

When Andre walked out of the clinic, he saw Destiny for the first time. She pulled on the car door handle and readied to climb in and drive away the moment she spotted Andre, who stared at her. Andre didn't hesitate. "'xcuse me. 'xcuse me!" He shouted as he quickly moved toward her. Destiny nervously crawled into her car. "Wait! Wait!" Andre continued. "I just want to know if you have the same allergy as me."

Destiny sheepishly said, "What makes you think I have an allergy?"

Andre turned toward the clinic and read, "Indianapolis Clinic for Allergies, and you are not wearing medical attire."

Andre stood beside her car door and said, "I have food allergies." Destiny put her hand to her forehead and laughed at herself. The fact that they might have something in common made her relax.

She moved her hand to her chest and said, "I have exercise-induced asthma from allergies. I come here for treatment." For the first time, she smiled at Andre.

Andre searched for something to say but was nervous. He blurted out, "My god, you are beautiful."

Embarrassed, Destiny said, "You don't know anything about me."

He smiled and said, "I'd like to."

"I don't know anything about you."

"I'm harmless."

"That's what all the serial killers say."

She made him laugh. His laugh delighted her. He saw that she had warmed up to him. "How about we go get a drink?"

She considered it. "Where do you work?"

"I'm an assistant math professor at the University of Indianapolis."

She knew the school well; her mother worked there. She offered, "There's a nice student bar on the edge of the campus. I could meet you there. Maybe we could get to know each other better."

"Yeah?" he smiled and laughed. "I'd like that. Go there next?" he asked.

"Wait," she said. "Do you have your own car?" She didn't want a stranger getting into her car.

He pointed to an old Buick, "Right over there."

She thought *he must not make much money as an assistant professor*, but she wanted to know more about him. "Okay, I'll meet you there in an hour. I need to drop some things off at home."

Over drinks, their relationship raced forward like Man o' War on a dirt track. They married within three months. A match made in heaven? Hardly, after a half year, Destiny left Andre. She found a roommate and decided to live a single life.

Olivia, a longtime friend, sought to help Destiny, who knew Olivia counseled people in all sorts of matters. She leaned on her friend for advice. Sure that she could help, Olivia often met with her friend over many drinks. She returned home drunk several nights after talking with Destiny. While her guidance helped Destiny find ways to reconcile with Andre, it stressed her marriage with Tom. Tom tried to understand the best he could. Even though he had no problem cooking for himself, the long and frequent visits with Destiny bothered him. He felt the discussions dragged Olivia down into Andre's and Destiny's problems.

One night Olivia returned from a drunken counseling session, and Tom waited patiently at the kitchen table. Drunk but not debilitated, Olivia hung the car keys on a rack near the door. She looked at Tom, who didn't say a word. She said, "Okay, okay. I'll pull back a little." She sorted through the mail. "'Sides, I think we made a breakthrough tonight. She will contact Andre and attempt to patch things up with him." She looked at Tom, whom she knew had been very patient. She even admired that he never pressed her for information on the other couple's business. She would never have told him anyway.

Tom scooted his chair sideways, patted his legs, and said, "Come here, lover."

Olivia sat, put her long arms around his neck, and gave him a big smooch.

August 2, 1998

That night, the two couples slept well, but Olivia woke early. She snuck out of bed, attempting to let Tom sleep. She slipped out the cabin's front door in her robe and slippers and looked for the newspaper, which the casino had arranged for daily delivery. She picked it up and thought about the paper delivery service. *Sometimes it's the little things that count.* She made her way to the kitchen and smiled as she turned on the

44

sink water because it poured out of the mouth of a fake skull. *This place is something else.*

At home, she heated the water with an electric kettle, but on vacation, she used the microwave to heat her water for tea. She had not yet noticed the big headline in the newspaper about a missing man. She reached into the cabinet for tea bags. The label read, P-O-I-S-O-N Tea. She read the rest of the warning to herself, "Drink at your own risk. This tea is poisoned with special herbs, blueberry flavors, and overdosed with caffeine." Shaking her head, she laughed at the poison warning. she said, "They have thought of everything!" Even so, she hesitated for a moment before drinking the tea.

She sat at the garish dining table and thought, *When they designed this table, they didn't consider its impact on a person with a slow morning start. It's more of an evening thing.* She brushed that thought aside and began to examine the newspaper. Her eyes widened, and she moved the paper closer to her face and read, "Man Missing from Local Home."

She read the story with interest to find out more about the home. She shook her head when she read the name of the home. Placid Place. She gulped down some tea. She had seen that place on the short drive between the bodega and the casino cottages.

"Watch ya' readin'?" Andre almost shouted as he entered the dining room.

Olivia jumped because of the sudden, noisy intrusion and because the story spooked her. Seconds later, Destiny and Tom entered the dining room. As Tom moved toward the kitchen, Olivia read some of the article out loud. "An old man was stolen from the Placid Place Home just down the street from here."

Andre said, "Maybe he fell into the 'placid lake' and drowned."

"It doesn't read as if they suspect drowning. The article indicates the man disappeared while on a shopping excursion away from the Home."

"You can't just steal someone from a group Home on an excursion like that. Hey, Destiny, bring on the mocha joe. What else does it say?"

From the kitchen, Destiny harrumphed and said, "You'll get whatever I bring you."

Olivia said, "All they say here, except that he is missing, is a description in case anyone finds him. He's about 5 feet 11 inches, white, has green eyes, and partially balding with white hair on the sides. He was last seen wearing blue jeans, a red t-shirt, and silver-rimmed glasses."

"That could be any old man in this part of Southern Indiana," Andre said as he took a cup of coffee from Destiny. "Okay, okay, I get it. Olivia will play detective every step of the way to the casino and back. She'll probably interrogate every ol' white guy."

Tom smiled at Olivia. Her penchant for involving herself in other's problems was well-known by the other three. It endeared her to him, even if his needs sometimes came in second to her desire to help others. "Well, I'm taking my tea back to our room to clean up and get dressed. I'm ready for breakfast and betting. How about you guys?"

Sluggishly, they agreed and made their way to their rooms.

Under the house, in a hidden cooling room, Jeck played with a pair of silver-rimmed glasses. Next to him, the missing old man whimpered with his hands tied behind his back. Jeck didn't waste time gagging him. Jeck knew no one would hear him if he shouted. He inspected the man. He sensed the old man as too weak to put up much of a fuss. Jeck had made sure the sound traveled one-way through the microphones hidden upstairs and speakers downstairs. The heavy soundproofing between floors ensured privacy for Jeck and his captive. Jeck reached out to the old man and poked a crooked finger into the man's shoulder. The man cried. His messy hair and wide open, wild, green eyes gave him the look of a lunatic, even though he stared at the lunatic who poked him. Jeck easily stole the old man away in front of everyone at the shopping center. He approached a bent-over man, leaning on his cane, and told him, "You look tired! Let's take you home." The exhausted man readily followed Jeck, who had him by one arm and guided him to Jeck's car.

The man eagerly climbed into the passenger's seat. He knew this wasn't the Placid Place Home's vehicle, but he barely contained his excitement about going to his own home. He thought Jeck intended to take him there. Years of loneliness, neglect from his extended family, and wishing to see his old home mistakenly drove him to follow Jeck. As Jeck shifted the car into drive, the old man looked at him and said with a whisper, "I'm really going home!" He sat next to Jeck with a broad grin on his face.

Below the main floor, Jeck asked, "What shall I do with you?" He feigned as if he cared what the man thought. "Should I let you go, you scared little rabbit?" Jeck's neck tensed as he moved closer to the old man. "Like that's going to happen. Ha! I smell the fear." He noticed that man pissed himself. "I love the smell of fear, especially with a little urine accentuating it. These things take time." He tapped the old man on the nose. "I'll warn you that you'll get very, very thirsty and hungry over the next couple of days. Sorry about your luck."

Jeck stood and towered over the frightened man. This morning, he had heard the entire conversation when Olivia read the story about this missing man. "No, no, no, you stay here while I get ready to follow them to the casino." Jeck smiled a crooked smile while pointing to the main floor.

Chapter 6 Sunday, August 2

As Tom predicted, Olivia stared at every white-haired, balding man as they walked to the casino. Andre pipped in, "Oh no, we aren't starting that again."

"Leave her alone," Destiny scolded. "It's her thing, and it won't hurt you." Tom nodded but didn't say anything. He knew Olivia would imbue herself into the situation even if it led nowhere. A couple of times, Tom also looked around, but not for a white-haired, balding man. Instead, he looked for something that made his hair stand on the back of his neck.

He paused and put a hand on Olivia's shoulder, "I feel like someone is following us."

Destiny laughed, "So the Murder & Mystery cabin is getting to tough, ol' Tom."

Tom thought about it. "Maybe.... I don't know. It just feels weird today."

Jeck walked well behind them. Following them qualified as child's play to Jeck. They made a ruckus wherever they went with their banter. Besides, following four people in his own backyard didn't challenge him. He felt disappointed in the lack of a challenge but enjoyed the sexual displays of the two women.

After breakfast and two hours of gambling, Andre observed Jeck staring at Destiny. Jeck looked pensive for the first time since they had arrived at the casino. He tapped one hand into the open palm of the other. He started to walk toward Destiny, stopped, stepped away, and then turned back toward her. Overcoming his apprehension, Jeck, unaware of Andre, finally walked up to Destiny. She shied away from Jeck and recognized that Andre had moved up to intercept him.

"Back off, creep," Andre said, putting a hand on Jeck's chest. Jeck quickly grabbed Andre's outstretched arm, twisted it, and pushed Andre away. Jeck's strength surprised Andre, something he wouldn't let happen again. Destiny shrieked and caught the attention of everyone in the room, including security.

Jeck and Andre's shouting and shoving match escalated until Jeck saw two security guards approach them. Andre, who faced the opposite direction, didn't see the guards. Jeck's face turned bright red with anger, but he quickly turned and ran out of the casino.

Andre shouted, "You'd better run fucker! You leave my woman alone!" The guards approached Destiny and Andre as Jeck headed out the door."

"Are you okay?" One of the security guards asked.

Andre blurted out, "You had better keep your clients away from my woman." Destiny glanced at Andre and thought, *I have to put an end to this, 'my woman' thing later.'* For the moment, she collected herself and turned toward the two guards.

"Yes, yes, we are fine. Just a little misunderstanding."

Andre asked, "Who is that creep?"

The second security guard said, "He comes in here a lot. He's normally harmless. The biggest issue is that he never spends any money when he wanders around. Management doesn't like that much, but there's nothing we can do about it."

"What's his name?" Andre asked.

"He calls himself Jeck. That's all we've been able to get out of him."

"Where does he live?"

"We don't know that, but we could not tell you even if we knew. That's private information."

Chapter 7

After the incident at the casino, the group proceeded to drink heavily. Tom's gambling efforts paid well for a second day, so he splurged on expensive champagne and all the drinks the others wanted. Destiny and Andre told Olivia and Tom about the incident, even though they had different perspectives. Andre portrayed the incident as an attack. Destiny saw the approach as an affirmation of her beauty. She felt sorry for Jeck, who, at first, timidly approached her.

"Hees...ish harmless," she slurred and hiccupped from the bubbly champagne.

"No, he isn't," Andre interjected.

"Guys ap... approach me all the time." She smiled with that confession.

"They should stay away from my woman."

Destiny, feeling the alcohol more than anyone, lit up. "Listen, buster, we are married, but I'm not your woman!"

Andre considered her words and attempted to decide where to go from there. She had admonished him before about this, and he had tried to back off from labeling her as such. Finally, he said, "But Honey, I love you so much."

"So why do you speak diminutively to me?"

Andre felt being quiet was his best defense at that moment. Tom and Olivia, feeling no pain because of the alcohol, also stayed silent.

After a few more minutes, Destiny said, "L-let's just forget about this incident and go back to the cabin and have a bonfire."

Olivia said, "Do you realize how hot it is?"

"Okay, skinny-dipping, and when it cools down tonight, we can do a bonfire."

Tom asked, "How about going back, taking a nap, skinny-dipping, and building a fire?"

Olivia nodded.

Alcohol possessed Destiny at this point. She smirked, "I like that idea! Can you take a nap with me, Tom? I'll let you get a little sleep."

Olivia chuckled. She knew Destiny was really drunk. Tom smiled but lowered his head to hide the smile.

Andre did neither. He grabbed Destiny by the arm and said, "You are completely out-of-your-mind drunk, woman."

"But I'm not YOUR woman." She pointed a long finger at his nose. "I'm your wife."

Andre slowly moved her hand from his face. "Let's just go back."

Olivia helped Destiny stand up, and the four returned to the cabin.

Because of her nap, Destiny sobered a little. The four dressed for swimming, with robes but no swimsuits. Andre delayed their swim. He asked, "Has anyone seen my Omega Seamaster graphite and black-faced wristwatch?"

Dressed in robes and ready to swim, the others were flustered. Destiny, almost in an apologetic way for her earlier behavior, put a hand on his shoulder. "No, baby, but we are going swimming. You don't need your watch right now."

To Andre, that was blasphemy. He brought three watches from his expensive collection, and one was missing. "I don't care about swimming until I find that watch."

Exasperated, the other three took separate rooms and began the search for Andre's watch. An hour later, Destiny pleaded with Andre. "You know the best way to find something lost is to quit looking for it."

"Do you know how much that cost me? I'm still making payments on it." Andre looked perturbed.

She reached out again and straightened the collar on his robe. "Honey, I know, but we've looked for an hour. Let it go for a while. We will swim and then come back and look more."

Andre gave in but knew the watch would be on his mind the entire time they swam. The watch cost him more than $2,000, and he just added it to his collection.

Relieved, Destiny, Olivia, and Tom headed for the lake while Andre reluctantly followed behind.

Once in the lake, Olivia effortlessly floated on her back with her arms lazily propelling her nowhere. "What is it about fresh lake water that calms the soul?" The others didn't answer because they knew Olivia had set herself up to provide that answer. "I believe it is the scent of good, clean lake water. It's the smell of the earth in liquid form. Yes, there's some decay of cattails or water lilies, but that's the process of the earth interacting with water that by itself has no scent. When I smell lake water, I feel peacefully primal."

Tom, who floated alongside Olivia, smiled, lost in her description of their present situation. "You have a way of putting me at peace, my dear."

Normally, Jeck would have observed the swimmers from his post in the briarwood, but today he contentedly sat in the hidden basement playing with Andre's watch.

He polished it with the older man's shirt. Jeck observed it closely while the old man felt sweat roll down his face. Jeck had never seen a watch such as this. "It's still a little dirty." It wasn't. He put the watch in front of the old man's face. "Spit on it." A cry mouth made it impossible for the man to work up a spit. Jeck looked at him as if he would kill him if he didn't. But then Jeck began to smile. He noticed the old man had pissed himself more. Jeck pulled the man's underwear up, giving him a frontal wedgie. "There we go. That will do it. Dousing the watch, Jeck used the man's shirt to polish and wipe the urine off the watch. "This is the best. I have the best watch in the whole world." He turned away from the man and stretched his arms up as if to touch the sky, even though he stood in a basement. When Jeck turned back to look at the man, the old man gasped, and his face turned white. Jeck leaned his head to the left as he watched life leave the old man's face. Jeck had seen this before and, without remorse, said, "Well, that's that." Jeck left the old man's body in the cold storage room.

Chapter 8 Peru, Indiana 1969

The carnie couple, who thought they had purchased one baby at the carpark in Germany, immediately found they had two babies for the price of one. It warmed their hearts, not because they loved babies, but because they gained two laboring sons.

They named them Hidel and Jeck. The couple decided on first names only. They didn't want to share their surname with the boys. Although they were twins, from the beginning, Hidel allowed Jeck to dominate him. At times Jeck would beat on him, and at other times Jeck protected Hidel like a parent protects a child. They developed a love-and-hate relationship that lasted the rest of their lives. Their adoptive parents made it worse with large helpings of cruelty. The torrid family situation drew the ire of the carnival owners in Germany. The young brothers often tussled, which caught the attention of carnival visitors. The Berlin Crisis of 1961 spilled over into the German economy and affected circus receipts. When layoffs occurred, the carnival owners chased the family away.

The carnie parents had read about an opportunity in Peru, Indiana. In the late 1800s and up to the great depression, Peru was the winter home for carnies in the United States. With shrinking profits for the Peru carnival company during the Great Depression, a Florida company bought the Peru outfit. The state of Florida took over as the carnival king.

Not to be put entirely away, entrepreneurs from Peru started a school for young and future carnies. In the 1960s, Peru became the amateur circus capital of the world. At its height, hundreds of young people with hopes of joining the circus, whether they had the talent or not, attended training in Peru. Not all talent abilities mattered if someone paid the tuition, and enough talent showed up to put on an amateur circus. Thousands of people attended the Circus City Festival. From Germany, the couple saw this carnie school as their opportunity to reign the boys in, so they fled to the town in Indiana, known as a refuge for carnival people.

Even in the circus world, the German parents stood out. Most of the other carnies saw their cruel and unusual treatment of Hidel and Jeck. They treated the two boys horribly, which spanned from making them hand clean the horse and elephant stalls to physically beating them for no reason. Most notable was the whip that their adopted father always carried. As mean as he could be in front of others, he never used the whip on the boys in public. But every evening before bed, he threatened the boys and cracked the whip on their backs for no reason. Each twin reacted differently. Jeck's face grew red with rage, and the platysmal bands bulged up in his neck as he turned to face his father in a rage. He resisted acting on his anger for a few years. Hidel, just the opposite, cowered under the abuse of the only man he knew as his father. He shivered and yelped with every thrust of the whip. When finished, Hidel crawled into his bed and hid under the blankets. Jeck stomped to bed and paced back and forth in his room as he plotted to end this affair.

Chapter 9 Peru, Indiana 1973

Sirens roared toward Jeck and Hidel's home as the house fire flamed into the sky. The flames offered some respite while Jeck and Hidel stood outside in the cold Indiana winter while their adoptive parents roasted in bed, not awakened by the fire. Jeck ensured they wouldn't wake before he set the house on fire. Many of the carnies believed Jeck had started the fire, but the authorities couldn't prove it. The carnival community spurned Jeck and Hidel. The authorities separated them and took them to different detention centers where the two boys awaited deportation. Because Jeck and Hidel entered the United States illegally with their foster parents, authorities sought ways to send them back to Germany. That process was a bureaucratic nightmare that separated the twins for almost two years. Jeck spent most of that time in trouble with the authorities. Hidel spent most of his time in seclusion and not interacting with others. The underpaid and underappreciated authorities left Hidel alone, not because they felt he needed alone time, but because they didn't care.

In the fall of 1975, Jeck hid in a crate headed for the landfill. Hiding involved Jeck crawling into the trash piled inside a container. He burrowed into the mixture of paper and garbage in the middle of the night. He waited until the morning when a trucker moved the container onto a flatbed truck and drove to the landfill. Hiding was easy. The container, no longer of value, slid off the back of the flatbed truck as the driver raised the bed with a hydraulic lift. The hauler drove away clueless about what he dumped into the landfill. When the truck bed raised and the crate slid off the back, Jeck slid face-first into the trash at the dump. As a precaution, Jeck stayed in that position until well after dark. Finding some edible garbage, he grabbed it and shoved it into his mouth. He searched for and found a ragged jacket and then sneaked out of the landfill confines with minimal security issues.

Before this daring escape, Jeck had broken into his detention center's main office and found records of where they held Hidel. During a twenty-five-mile walk, Jeck stole fresh clothes from a store in the middle of the night and cash from the store's register. He couldn't believe the owners had left that much cash in the register drawer. When he reached the town where they kept Hidel, he slept on a bench outside the center and waited for nightfall. No one questioned him or seemed to care that a youngster was sleeping on an outdoor bench. After dark, with the cunning of a master thief, he snuck into the center, found Hidel, and pulled him away. Hidel tried to fight

him, but Jeck dominated, and the two escaped into the night.

Chapter 10 1975

At twelve, the twins moved across Indiana from town to town, often homeless; they begged and sometimes were taken in, primarily by strange folks. Usually, their stays were abusive, either by a deviant patriarch or a drunken matriarch. Twice they lived in communes that were as different as two worlds apart. One commune housed farmer-types who eked out a living eating stable foods grown mainly in Indiana. The second existed with faux spiritualism, where they did drugs and ate canned and frozen foods that one hippy's parent paid for dearly.

The former commune stay ended when Jeck became abusive to Hidel, who accepted the treatment because it reminded him of his parents. The members of the conservative commune didn't accept it. They gave the boys an ultimatum. They faced being expelled or reported to child-protection service. Jeck never wanted to go down that path again, so he quietly led Hidel away from the commune.

For days on the road in southern Indiana, they walked and hitched rides to another Indiana burg known for its hippie-like commune. Jeck hoped for the best. He struggled and fought the urge to beat Hidel. The eventual beating went to another. A young girl about the same age as the boys attempted to build a relationship with Jeck. She was beautiful and stirred something in Jeck that he'd never experienced. He didn't know what to call it, but it made his compass stand up. He wanted more of the girl. The two agreed to meet in the middle of the night in a wooded area. The dark cloud cover hid their walk into the woods. They talked only for a few minutes until Jeck became sexually aroused. He began to stroke her in places no one had touched her. She asked him to stop, not because she didn't enjoy the physical pleasure but because Jeck smelled. Jeck attempted to force himself on her, but she quietly and amazingly held him off.

"Wait! Wait!" She whispered into his ear.

"What? Why?" He responded. He pushed her slightly, causing her to fall on her back.

She recovered quickly, sat up, put a hand on his crotch, and rubbed him. Living in a hippie commune, she understood what might take place, but this close to him, she couldn't stand how Jeck smelled. She recoiled and then realized she had a solution. With one hand on his chest, holding him back, she reached into a tiny carry bag and pulled out a bottle of Patchouli oil. Without warning, she sprinkled it on Jeck and giggled quietly.

Jeck's response was instantaneous and unexpected. In the dim light, his right arm arched at his side, and he slugged the girl in the head. She collapsed like a broken flower. Unconscious, she never heard Jeck yell at her. "Never spray me with anything." He winced and shook his hands, "Especially with something this fowl smelling." Despite Patchouli oil repulsing him, the silent and seemingly lifeless girl still aroused Jeck. He looked in all directions, slipped up her skirt, and planted his member into a girl for the first time. Even so, she didn't come around, and he made quick business of it. Soon, he stood over her still body. He reached down and felt for a pulse, as he had done with Hidel after many beatings. He considered what to do when he discovered she still lived. "This won't do. This won't do." He repeated. He banged his head with the palms of his hand. "What to do? What to do?"

He left the girl lying in the woods. He ran and retrieved Hidel. Again, the two would find their way on Indiana's back roads.

The girl woke in the dark with a bruised jaw and soreness she had never known. She wandered back to her foster parents and described all that she knew. The mother attempted to take care of her bruise. The father, stoned out of his mind, said, "Welcome to adulthood. That will teach you all about men." The couple didn't report it because the commune possessed too many illicit drugs. As far as the rest of the world knew, the girl's rape story ended that night. For the girl, she would never approach a man again for the rest of her life.

In a few days, while begging on the street, an elderly couple took Jeck and Hidel into their house. They allowed them to clean themselves and fed them. Their voracious appetites unhinged as the boys ate everything the couple brought them. After some discussion between themselves, the couple took the boys into their home. Jeck knew they had a lot of money hidden in the house, but he didn't know where. It took him a few weeks, but he finally realized he did not sleep on a regular mattress stuffing and bedsprings. He clawed at the mattress until he could poke two fingers into it. He squeezed his fingers on a piece of paper and pulled out a one-hundred-dollar bill. In his excitement, he immediately showed it to Hidel, who had no comprehension of what the one-hundred-dollar bill was worth. His face showed his cluelessness.

Jeck said, "This will buy our freedom."

The excitement unhinged Jeck. He saw the first absolute freedom for himself and his brother. He figured old methods were the best, but instead of waiting outside the burning home, they ran off during the night. They carried pillow slips stuffed with one-hundred-dollar bills.

The move from town-to-town tortured Hidel. He only wanted to hide. Each new town, with different people, scared and scarred his mind and soul. Still, Jeck dragged him from town to town. With every stop, Hidel burrowed into the next abandoned building.

Chapter 11 August 2, 1998

While Jeck and the others in the cottage slept, Hidel played with the wristwatch. He admired the beauty of the small trinket, even though he didn't know its purpose. It intrigued him. Instead of reacting like Jeck and thinking he held the most beautiful item in the world, he felt guilty that Jeck stole it from its owner. To Hidel, the next step was simple. Return it.

The process took an hour. Hidel took each step up the hidden staircase at moments per step. He didn't want to risk waking Jeck. When he reached the secret door to the main floor, he took minutes to open it. He hoped the hinges would not squeak. They didn't. If someone saw this from inside the main floor, it looked like the wall moved by itself. This was the fake door with the evil eye Tom had found on the main floor the day they explored the house's unique features. Jeck had designed the door frame so that someone on the main floor thought it opened into a wall. Inside the hidden vertical shaft, Hidel had unlocked the secret wall and then the door frame very carefully. *Very clever, Jeck*, Hidel thought. Once inside the main floor, Hidel took his time to walk to the refrigerator. Instead of invading Andre and Destiny's bedroom where they were sleeping, he decided to put the thing in the fridge. He hoped that Andre would think it fell there. When he opened the fridge, he almost gasped out loud. He had never seen so much food. The food and beverages stuffed the refrigerator to the point he was unsure where to put the watch. Hidel committed his life to keeping his personal feelings and reactions to himself, except with Jeck; as such, he didn't gasp verbally, but he did mentally. Carefully, he put the watch on top of a beer bottle sitting on the back of the second shelf.

With the same commitment to silence, Hidel returned to the hidden basement.

August 3

The next morning, Destiny opened the refrigerator to grab the orange juice. She smirked when she saw the wristwatch through the glass shelf sitting on the beer bottle below it. Whispering to herself, she said, "Who would have thought to look into the refrigerator." Forgetting the orange juice, she picked up the watch.

Sitting on the bed next to sleeping Andre, she waved it back and forth until the motion of her body woke Andre. His eyes opened wide, and he quickly reached up for the watch. "Where did you find this?"

"Probably right where you dropped it. On a beer bottle in the refrigerator."

Andre contemplated that fact. "But wait, I drank beers after I lost it. Why didn't I see it then?"

"Because you were drunk!" Destiny exclaimed. "Okay, I will say that it was on the last bottle in the back. I only saw it because it was under the orange juice."

Still confused, Andre smiled and said, "Thank you, baby. This is one of my favorite watches."

"Well, that's good to hear, so you're not going to mope all day about losing it?"

"You bet I won't."

Jeck woke to Destiny s words through the speakers in the basement. Hidel sat in his bed and waited for Jeck's response. Jeck gave him an incredulous look, then jumped up and went to where he had left the watch. It wasn't there.

Jeck walked back to Hidel. They both knew what would happen next. Jeck's fist slammed against Hidel's face so hard it sounded as if Hidel's jaw broke. Then, Jeck beat the hell out of him.

Chapter 12 August 3

Amazingly, Hidel survived the beating and retreated to hide under the covers in his bed. Jeck didn't speak to him or help him. Most importantly, he quit bringing him food. That didn't bother Hidel. He remembered where he could get all the food he wanted. After dark, he returned to the refrigerator with the same stealth as the night before.

Standing in the kitchen, he realized that the two couples were outside around the bonfire. He also saw Jeck spying on the couples from the briarwood. He grabbed two handfuls of pizza, the last of that pizza, from the refrigerator, walked to one of the barred windows, and watched them party around the fire. The foursome laughed, told jokes, drank beer, and sucked on a bourbon bottle. Hidel imitated the motion of drinking a beer, never having drunk one. He then feigned a smile as if he was one of the happy guests. The act of smiling reminded him that Jeck nearly broke his jaw. He knew he must do something to appease him. An idea came to him. He snuck into Andre and Destiny's bedroom. He looked through a couple of drawers until he found a pink bra. Instinctively, he held it to his nose and sniffed it. *This will make Jeck happy.*

He began to return to the downstairs apartment. As he did, he crossed another window. He looked at the happy couples one more time.

That's when Olivia saw him.

The firelight lit up the bedroom window, and Hidel stood frozen for a moment looking at Olivia. She jumped up. "Oh my god, someone is in your bedroom, Destiny." Hidel quickly moved to the hidden door and retreated to his bed.

The other three argued with Olivia. Tom said, "We've been here all night, and no one has come and gone from our cabin. It's the firelight playing tricks on you. Sit down and enjoy your beer."

Olivia pointed toward the cabin, "Hell no! I saw someone."

Tom rolled his eyes.

"I'm not going to settle down, but I'm not going in there to search without you."

Andre and Destiny shrugged and didn't intend to move. Olivia stared at Tom and demanded, "Come on, Tom. Let's go look."

Tom dutifully followed Olivia. Destiny shrugged, "If they are going to our room, we might as well go." The four walked back into the cabin and slowly opened the front door.

Jeck used that time to return to the basement to find Hidel.

Olivia turned on every light as she passed by the switches. When they entered Andre and Destiny's bedroom, even before Olivia switched on the light, Tom said, "Do you really think someone would still be in here after you screamed and pointed to this window?" Once Olivia turned on the light, they studied the room and thought it looked undisturbed.

Tom said, "Honey, the firelight played a trick on you."

Olivia gave him a stern look as if to say, *I know what I saw.* Then shaking her head, "We are going to search every square inch of this place." She didn't know that was impossible because of the hidden rooms.

In the basement, Jeck and Hidel listened to the two couples bicker about someone being in the cabin.

Jeck looked suspiciously at Hidel. "What did you do?"

Hidel looked at the floor but raised his head when he brought his left hand from behind his back and handed Jeck Destiny's pink bra. Jeck immediately knew it was a peace offering from his brother. Slowly he reached out for it, and instinctively, like Hidel, he pulled it toward his nose. He took in Destiny's scent. Unabashedly, he rubbed his face in it and thought of Destiny. After a few moments, Jeck looked at Hidel and said, "You are forgiven."

Hidel tried to smile like he had seen the others doing just a few minutes ago. His smile was broken, partially because he didn't know how and partially from Jeck beating on him, not just today but every day since they began so long ago.

The two couples combed the cabin but found no clue of an invader. After twenty minutes, Andre said, "We've searched and found no one. I agree with Tom; the fire played a trick on you. Let's grab fresh beers and go back out to the fire."

While the others dismissed the intruder, Olivia exclaimed, "I know what I saw. I know what I saw."

Andre smirked and waved her off as he reached for a beer. As simple as his motion was, it hurt Olivia. He also looked for the last two slices of pizza. "Hey, what happened to the pizza?

Destiny said, "It should be in there."

"Well, it's not." Andre opened his beer and proceeded to forget about the pizza.

Tom cocked his head to one side, shrugged his shoulders, gave Olivia a look, and said, "Give it up, babe." Olivia sat at the table as the other three returned to the bonfire. After a few minutes of fighting the fear and resenting how the others treated her, she hesitantly joined them by the fire. She didn't want to be in the cabin alone. Because an intruder might still be in the house, her fear grew, and she didn't know if she could maintain control.

When she sat in a lawn chair by the fire, Tom patted her on her well-tanned leg and said, "Hey, you got your freak on staying at this place. Isn't that what you wanted?"

Olivia sat quietly, thinking about what she saw.

Chapter 13 1996 Rising Sun, Indiana

The first casino built in Indiana was on the Ohio River outside Rising Sun. State legislators, for whatever reason, required that a casino float on water. Later, the state's gifted thinkers said the casino could be permanently docked. While the riverboat casino laws intended to be restrictive, they enhanced the gambling experience. For nostalgic reasons, if nothing else, people enjoyed gambling on a riverboat, even with a permanently docked boat. That worked well for the Rising Sun Casino.

Through all their travels, Jeck and Hidel wound up in Rising Sun. Jeck, always the adventurous one, attended the casino. Hidel, as usual, hid in the deserted house that Jeck found for them.

Good luck never played a big part in the brothers' lives until they visited Rising Sun. Jeck placed a one dollar bet on a slot machine and won $432,000. The casino patrons went wild. The win ranked as the highest one-dollar payout from an Indiana casino at that time. Cheers came from everywhere. Jeck didn't like that because he didn't want to attract attention. The casino managers invited him into the back office to discuss the matter. They soon found out that he was an illegal alien. This created quite a stir for the casino managers. After phone calls to the owners, management decided to keep this situation under control and hidden from the public.

Jeck didn't want to give out personal information and especially didn't want to have his picture taken for a press release. Instead, he and the management agreed to a settlement. Jeck was given one thousand dollars cash and asked to return in two days to receive $200,000 in cash and sign off on the rest. When he returned in two days, he learned something that changed his and Hidel's life.

A display in the casino showed the future of gambling in Indiana. Jeck learned that the Rising Sun casino owners planned a new concept in gambling. They called it 'Bets and Breakfasts.' They designed a riverboat casino on the Ohio River, near Louisville, KY but on the Indiana side. This new casino also featured themed cottages within walking distance. The cabins sat on a sprawling 640-acre wooded area along the Ohio River. The themed cottages included a fairy and elven house, an Elvis house, and an auto racing house in honor of the racing capital of the world in Indianapolis. Jeck learned there would be twenty-five themed houses, but the only one that intrigued him was the

Murder & Mystery cottage. He saw its plans in a collection of promotional materials at the Rising Sun Casino.

Something happened along the way. By the time the Murder & Mystery, Elvis, and Fairy and Elven Cottages were built, the new casino owners missed a few installments of payments on the operating loan. The riverboat casino and hotel stood beautiful and tall, but the grand opening didn't include the themed cottages. The three existing cabins sat vacant. Weeds grew tall in the empty construction lots around them. The owners boarded up the doors and windows to the cottages for months. Those months allowed Jeck and Hidel to break in and live in the Murder & Mystery cottage. Jeck used half of the money he had won to remodel the Murder & Mystery cottage basement. He added the black utility shed next to the briarwood and painted the window black. He and Hidel hand-dug the area for the stairs and tunnel into the cabin's basement. They hand-carried the dirt and rocks from the tunnel and dumped them into the lake. Jeck used the time he walked back and forth from the shack to the lake to plan the hideaway further. Hidel used the time to count the 16,000 steps per day. Once they dug into the cabin, they broke through the basement floor and created hidden rooms that would become their permanent living space.

Two years after the temporary stoppage, the casino owners regained the capital to build the twenty-two remaining themed cabins. Jeck learned that this part of the "Bets & Breakfasts" of the casino would open in early 1998. He immediately started installing hidden cameras and microphones and the acoustic insulation that divided the basement from the main floor as if they existed on separate continents.

When the themed cottage opened, they lived well in the hidden rooms, and Jeck came and went via the tunnel to the outer shed. They hid while guests stayed in the above-ground portion of the house. In the end, Jeck felt disappointed in the show that the boring guests provided. On the other hand, Hidel enjoyed the simplicity of watching people eat and talk while he hid in the basement.

Chapter 14 Tuesday, August 4

Destiny began to think that the Murder & Mystery cabin was a mistake while she and the others walked to the casino for breakfast. She sensed a tension between them, unlike any of their other vacations. Instead of their vacation routines – of eating breakfast, gambling, drinking, swimming, and ending the night with a bonfire AND more drinking – being fun, they became routine to her. Instead of vacation activities occurring spontaneously, they plodded through them. Something more bothered Destiny. She hated to think of it, but somehow, she felt less trusting of the others, especially *her man* Andre. She tickled herself as she thought about him that way.

After a full day of the usual, the foursome relaxed by the fire for more drinking. She tried to broach her concern about everyone's behavior.

Andre jumped on it. "What are you talking about? Where have you been? We are getting along great, like usual."

Destiny folded her arms at Andre's opposition.

Olivia attempted to smooth it over. "I must agree with her. I'm thinking this place is getting to us."

Destiny jumped back into the conversation. "It's not the place. I think we are changing."

Tom held up his beer. "It might be our drinking. I think we've been drinking more than usual."

All four became silent and stared at the fire.

Destiny excused herself from the bonfire to go in and use the bathroom. In her bedroom, she realized that she hadn't worn her pink bra for a couple of days. She touched her breasts, knowing that Andre loved that bra. She rifled through the drawer but didn't find it. She looked through all the drawers. Hands on her hips, she thought, *Andre loves to play with her lingerie, but only with me in them. Surely Tom wouldn't come in and steal it*

After searching the entire cabin, she returned to the bonfire and the others. "Okay, who stole my pink bra?"

Olivia immediately looked at Tom. He almost spilled his beer that he had just sipped. Incredulously, Tom held out his arms with his hands in the air and looked at the three, "What? Why is everyone looking at me?"

Olivia folded her arms in front of her. "Sounds like you're the only one who might pilfer it."

"Well?" Destiny asked.

"First, I didn't steal it. Second," he looked at Olivia. "that's beneath me, and until now, I would have thought it was beneath you to think I might have."

Destiny said, "Who else would have stolen it." She froze in place and stared at the window.

Olivia chimed in. "Wait, I told you all that I saw someone in your bedroom window the other night."

Andre laughed and said, "Someone broke into our cabin and took nothing but Destiny's bra? Come on." He looked at Destiny. "You probably misplaced it." He laughed again and said, "Did you look in the fridge?"

Tom almost smiled at that comment but still mused about Olivia's accusation that he had stolen it. It hurt him to the core that she suddenly lacked trust in him.

Destiny frowned at Andre, "I'm going to bed." She turned to go inside but stopped. The thought that someone might be in the house frightened her. "Come with me, Andre," she demanded.

He held up his unfinished beer bottle.

Destiny stomped on her way back to the cabin. "Fine. Be that way!"

Olivia's jaw dropped, and she thought. *How can the night end poorly because of a missing bra?*

Chapter 15 Wednesday, August 5

The following day, they dismissed the events of the night before as drunken folly. Olivia and Destiny walked to the car and discussed what supplies they needed to pick up from the grocery store. Olivia wore a very short skirt. Destiny commented, "Who do you want to lure with that outfit?"

"Anyone I want!" She laughed devilishly but knew she wouldn't intentionally flirt with anyone. Like, Destiny, though, she enjoyed being sexy and putting on a show for anyone who might watch. Olivia climbed into the driver's seat while still chatting with Destiny. "It will be good to get away from the boys for a few hours."

"Yep, it's time for girl talk. Do you think Tom stole my bra?"

"With all his faults, he doesn't lie. He just doesn't know how to."

"Then what happened to my bra?"

"Good question."

While the camera wouldn't start until Olivia started the car, the microphone worked perfectly. Jeck and Hidel listened intently.

Destiny hesitated and thought about Andre always falling asleep right after he orgasmed. She blurted out, "Does Tom satisfy you sexually?"

"Now that's a personal question," she started to put the key into the ignition but hesitated. "Okay, what's up, girl? You know you can talk to me. I won't tell anyone."

"I know that about you, lordy; you've had plenty of stories to tell others about me. Okay, so here it is. Andre is great at making love…" she hesitated and looked directly at Olivia, who raised an eyebrow and wondered where she would go with that. Destiny added, "…for his pleasure." She snickered with embarrassment. "But when it comes to me, he's a no-show."

Olivia pointed the key at her and said, "That's a problem. Now, I see why you asked. Tom is very considerate and takes care of my every need if you know what I mean."

Destiny leaned back against the seat, rolled her eyes, and gasped.

Olivia added, "I've counseled you before. I know you love Andre." She hesitated and gestured with the car key while she thought. "You probably cannot change him. He must change himself. I suggest you see a marriage counselor this time for those two reasons." She hesitated but asked, "Why didn't you find that out before you married him?"

Destiny whimpered, "For religious reasons. Andre didn't want to have sex before we married. I respected his opinion, and it kind of endeared me to him."

"Well, we make our own beds, so we have to sleep in them. Speaking literally in this case." Olivia looked somberly at Destiny, turned toward the steering wheel, put the key in the ignition, and proceeded to start the vehicle. Nothing happened. The car was silent.

Destiny said, "That's weird."

"Yeah, this car has been so reliable."

Destiny opened her door, walked to the back of the car, and looked at the tailpipe. She shook her head and returned to the open passenger door. "It's not the exhaust. I've seen many comedies and mystery shows where someone blocked the exhaust so a car wouldn't start. That's something one of the boys might have done."

Standing outside the car, she bent down to look at Olivia. "Hey, what's that?" She pointed next to Olivia's left foot. Moving her foot, Olivia reached down and picked up a fuse.

Destiny said, "Now that's weird. How could an ignition fuse just fall out like that?"

Hidel lightly poked Jeck on the shoulder. "Way to screw that up." Hidel cowered as if he should not have said anything.

Jeck's response surprised Hidel. "No harm. No foul. They won't suspect anything."

Olivia twisted and moved her legs out of the car so Destiny could replace the fuse. Knowing cars so well, Destiny didn't look under the dash. She felt her way to where a fuse was missing and snapped it back into place. She looked at Olivia and said, "Try it now."

Still sitting sideways, Olivia turned the key and started the car. She smiled, looked at Destiny, and said, "You are a genius."

Instantly, the hidden camera started. Jeck and Hidel weren't disappointed as Olivia slid her long legs back into the car. They had been listening to the two women talk about their sex life. Hidel dreamed about the nights that Destiny pleasured herself while Andre snored, but then he glanced at Jeck and shook his head. "Well, you got lucky."

Jeck didn't listen to Hidel. Instead, he plotted what he would do with Andre.

The two girls drove away and headed for a grocery store. Neither the wireless microphone nor the camera range lasted. The brothers watched and listened as the monitors grew blank.

Chapter 16 August 5

Andre returned from the casino. He quit gambling because he had lost too much money. Tom waved goodbye to him and continued at the slot machine.

The cabin seemed spookier to Andre because he walked in alone. His heart thumped hard when he heard a loud bang in the backyard. He grabbed an umbrella from the stand and slowly stepped out the back door. Bang! He listened to the sound again. Afraid but otherwise undeterred, he stepped toward the shed, where the banging continued.

Hidden by the shack, Hidel continued to slam a long and broken branch against the shack's back wall. The noise had captured Andre's attention so well that Jeck snuck up behind him and broke a branch over Andre's head. Andre had just about peered around the corner of the shack, where he would have seen Hidel when his lights went out. He fell to the ground. Jeck stood over him and said, "That'll teach you for not taking care of your beautiful wife. Some of us never get to touch that kind of beauty, let alone fuck it."

Hidel cried as he walked around the corner of the shack. He yelled, "You didn't have to hit him that hard."

Jeck considered Hidel's comment, stole the branch Hidel held, and threatened to hit him with it. Hidel cowered away from his brother. Jeck scanned the house to make sure no one saw them. He looked up into the tree. His timing had been perfect. Everyone would think the branch fell and knocked Andre out. Jeck threw Hidel's branch into the briarwood and motioned for both to retreat to the basement.

Then Jeck stopped. He turned around, walked up to Andre's prone body, and kicked him in the crotch.

Moments later, Andre woke with a splitting headache and a sore crotch. He rubbed the back of his head and winced. He had no clue where he was. Temporary amnesia overtook his mind. Destiny, who had returned with Olivia, looked out the kitchen window and saw Andre squatting on the ground. She dropped the jar she had just pulled out of the grocery sack. Beets and juice splattered all over the floor, her legs, and the cabinet.

Olivia shouted, "What the...?" She watched Destiny run out the back door and saw Andre on the ground. She pursued.

Destiny slid onto the ground next to Andre. "What happened, baby?" She watched him gingerly tough his noggin.

"She rose to her knees and looked at Andre's head. "You are bleeding. Run, get a clean cloth, Olivia."

Andre studied Destiny with a dazed look on his face. "Who are you?"

Destiny gasped and put a hand to her mouth. "I'm your wife?"

Olivia returned with a wet facial cloth and another with ice. Destiny looked at the broken branch, the tree above them, and reached for Olivia's ice pack. "It seems he has amnesia from the impact of this branch." She wanted to ask Andre why he was in the back of the house. Instead, she quietly held the ice pack on his head.

Andre considered his situation. He knew of amnesia and that two plus two equaled four. That part of his brain functioned. He looked at the branch and concluded that it had hit him. He also knew his crotch hurt but didn't attribute it to the branch. He gently reached for Destiny's thin arm. "I-I'm sorry," he muttered. Perplexed, Destiny looked sidelong at Andre."

"You don't have to be sorry? You are the one beaned by a falling branch."

"I-I don't know. I just have this weird feeling that I owe you an apology."

"Oh, baby, it's okay that you didn't recognize me. You've taken quite a hit."

Andre tensed his face. "It's not that." He squinted toward the bright sky. "It's coming back to me. We are on vacation. I came out here to investigate some noise and blacked out." He looked around, licked his lips, and said, "But there's something I'm supposed to be sorry for. I can't place it."

"Don't worry about that. Let's get you to the casino infirmary. Can you stand?"

Olivia and Destiny guided Andre around the house and into the car. Olivia said, "I'll stay here and put the cold and frozen groceries away. And clean up the mess."

Bewildered, not understanding why Andre wandered out behind the house, Olivia put the groceries away. After she swept up the broken glass from the fractured beet jar, she made a vinegar and warm water solution and applied it to the beat stains. Moments later, the kitchen cabinet and floor shined cleanly.

When Tom entered the dining room, Olivia sat with a hot tea in front of her at the dining table. Immediately, Tom saw the look of concern in her eyes. "What's up?"

Olivia slid the cup of tea toward Tom, offering him a sip. He sat, concerned for Olivia, and said, "Tell me, what is it?"

"It's the darndest thing. We returned from the store and found Andre on the ground, semi-conscious after a branch bashed him on the head." Tom started to stand. Olivia patted him on the arm. "It's okay; Destiny took him to the casino infirmary."

Tom pointed in the direction of the casino, "I just came from there. I didn't see them."

"They must have taken him into the infirmary before you left the slot machines."

Tom stood, walked to the kitchen fridge, opened it, and grabbed a beer. "I hope he's all okay."

Chapter 17 August 5

When Destiny returned with Andre, he walked into the cabin with a big grin. Olivia greeted them at the door and asked, "How are you?"

"I'm just effin' fine," Andre said and laughed, holding his ribs because he laughed so hard.

Destiny rolled her eyes and said, "It's the hydrocodone affecting him and…"

"And what?"

"I couldn't stop him. When we walked out of the infirmary, he waltzed up to the bar and slugged down two bourbons."

Tom said, "That's our Andre."

Olivia gave Tom a sidelong glance but then turned her attention to Destiny. "What did the medics say?"

"That he will be a pain in the ass for a few days," Destiny said.

Andre laughed so hard that he fell back against the wall. Tom reached for him. "Easy there, fellow."

Stammering, Andre blurted, "Did you hear the one about the judge who forgot the statue of laminations?"

"A thousand times, Honey," Destiny rolled her eyes.

Andre's memory had wholly returned. "Having your head hit is so much fun. You should try it sometime, Tom."

All three of the others furrowed their brows while looking at Andre.

Jeck and Hidel listened to Andre laugh. "Damn," Jeck said. "They dosed him so much; he's actually having a good time." Hidel again tried to smile like he'd seen the others do. "Wipe the stupid grin off your face," Jeck said while pointing at Hidel.

On the main floor, Andre reached into his pocket for pills. "I didn't mean knocked on the head. I meant these." He held the drugs in front of Tom.

Again, Olivia looked at Tom with concern about drugs in the house. Tom knew what she thought. Tom and Olivia met because she played basketball and he coached. While attracted to each other, they kept that relationship professional and didn't date. Life moved on for them both. Tom left coaching and took a very successful but tedious office job. The money and the crowd he associated with turned him toward drugs. Tom emersed himself in the drug culture. It didn't kill him. His job didn't suffer, but one of his friends died from a crug overdose. That event saved Tom's life.

1991

When Tom sought rehabilitation, Olivia greeted him. He never thought he'd see one of his former students in a rehabilitation meeting. Olivia smiled, "I became a counselor after I graduated." She reached out to shake Tom's hand. Shocked, Tom just stood and looked at her. She reached down, grabbed his hand, and shook it firmly. "I'm happy you came to our call-out meeting. We get to know everyone here." She motioned toward the room where fifteen people talked and waited for the meeting to start. "Do you want to join us?"

Tom's mind raced. He asked himself, 'Should I stay? Go?'

Olivia's presence, a former student, made him uneasy. Olivia could see that. "Why don't you have a seat? You did so much for me as a coach. It's my turn to help you."

Flee. Flee, he thought, but Olivia's presence also placed him back to when he was drug free. Instead of fleeing, Tom quietly sat on a chair by the exit. Moments turned into an hour. An hour turned into many more sessions. Sessions turned into a dinner; both felt uncomfortable with the situation but were passionate about it. The dinner turned into sex, and the two never looked back. Eventually, Tom became drug-free but not addiction free. Olivia became his addiction.

August 5, 1998

Andre broke their thoughtful silence. "Man, this shit is good. You should try this, Tom." He shook the prescription bottle that he held out for Tom. Andre knew about Tom's former drug addiction. Normally, he wouldn't have tempted Tom, but, well, he was high.

Tom raised a hand, and Olivia thought Tom might take the bottle. Instead, he said, "No, thank you, Andre, those days are behind me."

"Suit yourself."

Destiny scorned Andre with her eyes. She looked at Tom and Olivia. "Anyway, they looked him over, and he doesn't even have a concussion. The falling branch knocked him out and screwed up his marbles for a bit."

Tom joked, "Well, that's good to know. I'd hate to spend the rest of my vacation visiting Andre in some hospital."

Andre laughed as if it was the funniest thing he had ever heard.

Destiny smirked and pointed a thumb at Andre, "That may have been better than this for the next few days."

Chapter 18 August 5

After hours of non-stop drinking that evening, Destiny retreated to her upstairs bathroom and then to her bedroom to rest for a few minutes. The day overwhelmed her, so she turned to booze and one of the joints that Andre had bought. She closed her eyes, but that made her even more nauseous. She opened them again and stared up at the painting at the head of the bed. Her imagination gave her many options for what hid around the corner of the cave. "Stop that," she told herself. "Nothing is coming around the corner. It's just a painting."

She listened to the others chatting and laughing downstairs. A few minutes later, she decided to rejoin the group. She carefully descended the stairs, extended her long arms, and lightly slid her fingers that barely touched the walls. When she reached the second step, she thought an earthquake shook the cabin. Instead, the stairs collapsed into a slide. She fell on her derriere with her hand smacking the flat board that once made a staircase. Sliding the rest of the way down, she jumped up when her feet reached the landing. She turned and stared at the stairs that now looked like a slide. "How could that happen? Even though I am in a mystery house, I can't believe it." She found Andre in the kitchen. "You have to come with me." She commanded. Andre looked wide-eyed at Tom and Olivia and then looked at Destiny with a quizzical expression. He shrugged and said, "Okay. Where are we going?"

"To the staircase. It just collapsed on me."

Andre laughed and said, "You're not heavy enough to do that! It's the alcohol, dear." Olivia elbowed him in the ribs.

Intrigued, Tom, and Olivia followed. When they reached the staircase, it locked normal.

Andre laughed again and said, "Yep. It's the drinking."

Destiny protested. "No, it collapsed and became as flat as a slide. I fell on my rear. I think I bruised it." She reached for her derriere and pulled up the bottom of her shorts.

Tom ogled Destiny until Olivia covered his eyes with her hand. She then asked Destiny, "Are you okay?"

"I think so. I can't explain what happened, but I know the stairs collapsed."

Below the stairs, Jeck flashed a great big grin because of what his invention did. When he remodeled the cottage, he painstakingly built the steps so that he could trigger them to collapse into a slide. He played with Destiny remotely because of

his frustration that he couldn't physically touch her.

Chapter 19 August 6

Andre improved significantly overnight but still took the painkillers. He looked at Destiny, who didn't fight it because she figured the pain still pounded in his head. After twenty minutes, Andre giggled in delight.

Even though Andre had laughed at her falling the night before, Destiny worried about Andre gambling while on drugs. She said, "I'm going to keep an eye on your gambling today."

True to her words, she sat behind Andre at the poker table instead of enjoying the roulette wheel. Despite being doped up, Andre held himself together in the game, but while sitting at the poker table, the drugs made Andre remember a dumb joke. He stretched his hands out on the table, which made the others pause. "Did you hear that someone shot a person on the beach at the south end of the lake?" Thinking he was serious, the other card players indicated that they hadn't heard. "Well, don't worry, you're safe. The guy who got shot was barefoot and had no toes. It turns out the shooter was lack-toes-intolerant." Nobody laughed or even groaned except Andre, who laughed until he cried.

He let slip a few more dumb jokes until someone interjected, "Are you on drugs? Can we just get on with the game?"

Destiny said, "Turns out he is on drugs. A tree branch knocked him on the head yesterday. Please give him some slack."

The man responded, "Sure, with a fine piece of ass like you, we'll give him all kinds of slack."

Destiny moved away from the man and the poker table. Andre turned to look at her, and she was quite a site. Her beautiful skin shone through the light-colored tight tank top. Her legs flowed from her shorts, one of her favorite items to wear on hot August days. Her big, black eyes pierced into Andre's soul when she returned her gaze toward him. She raised her eyelids as if she would ask Andre why he turned to look at her. Instead, without realizing it, she turned to look at the crass man and saw that he still ogled her.

Slowly Andre turned toward the stranger, who had been losing a lot of money. He nodded toward the small pile of chips the man had in front of him. Andre said, "Looks like you should keep a closer eye on your hand than my woman."

With that comment, Destiny decided she didn't need to look over Andre anymore. She promptly walked to the roulette wheel. Andre began winning more, lost track of time, and didn't even notice when people came and went. Two hours later, he decided to cash in on his winnings. He passed by the roulette wheel, where he saw Destiny accepting a drink from the man from the poker game. The drug Andre was on didn't help him think clearly. Normally, he would have approached the two, sometimes, he might have punched the man, but this time he cashed in his chips and left the casino.

When Tom, Olivia, and Destiny wanted to leave the casino, they didn't find Andre.

Tom said, "That's strange."

Destiny replied that he had been temperamental all morning, "It's probably the drugs and the head injury. He might have walked back to the cabin."

Tom, who had looked for him in the Men's room, said, "We've searched enough here. Let's go back there. If we don't find him, I'll come back here. It isn't like him to disappear."

"As I said, he's not normally bonked on the head and taking drugs."

They found Andre sitting beside the bonfire in the heat of the day. Tom said, "Hey, bud, what are you doing here?"

He dismissively waved the back of his hand toward Destiny. "She didn't want me around. Instead, miss hot pants wanted to share a drink with another man."

Destiny lightly put her fingers to her throat. "OMG, Andre. I'm not going to turn down a free drink. The stranger bought me that drink because he wanted to apologize for his crass remark. I've been given hundreds of drinks over the years."

"I saw how he looked at you and how you looked at him."

Astonished, "He gave me the drink, apologized, thanked me for being beautiful, and left. There was nothing to it."

Tom and Olivia decided not to be a part of that tete-a-tete. They went indoors.

"There's no talking to you now. I looked out for you at the poker table, and this is how you treat me." Destiny put one arm in the air and pointed after Tom and Olivia. "I'm going into the air conditioning. You can sit out here and sweat your balls off."

Destiny walked into the kitchen, grabbed a beer from the fridge, and then sat at the dining table where she could keep an eye on Andre. Not satisfied, she stood, walked into the kitchen, poured a vodka, and slurped it down. On a hot day like that, she would have added ice, but she didn't want to wait.

Next to the fire, the more Andre thought about the situation; he foolishly wondered how many times Destiny accepted a drink from a stranger and what she did about it. The more he thought, the more he imagined Destiny cheating on him. The more he imagined Destiny cheating, the more he wanted to avoid her, even if it meant he had to sit by the fire in the heat of the day. That didn't help his head, and neither did the constant drinking.

While Destiny kept an eye on Andre, she poured more vodka for herself. She pulled two more glasses out of the cabinet for the other two. Olivia tried to resist, but Tom encouraged her. On the first sip, Tom said, "This vodka tastes different." He swirled the vodka in his glass. He pulled the vodka bottle from Destiny and inspected it. "My Gawd, this is wheat vodka. We must make sure Andre doesn't get any. It could kill him."

Destiny swirled her vodka in her glass, "It won't kill him, but it will make him very sick."

Several shots and beer later, the trio had drunk their way past dinner. Destiny went into great detail about Andre's allergies and explained what would make him sick and what would kill him. She looked out the window at Andre, still sulking by the fire.

Jeck had listened to her entire description of Andre's allergies.

"He can be so damn s-stubborn," Destiny slurred. At nightfall, she watched him sulk by the fire. "Ok...Okay, I'll grab a couple of beers and go out to him."

Tom stood up as if to join her, but Olivia put a hand on his arm. "Sit," she whispered. "Let them dual this out."

Destiny handed a beer to Andre and sat in the chair next to him. She didn't expect to hear what he had to say.

"SOOO, let me ask," Andre didn't slur, but he seethed from the anger that built up while he sat alone. "How many men have you slept with since we've been married?"

Destiny's jaw dropped. Her mind spun, and it felt like the distance between them physically grew. "What? How can you ask that? It's been zero!!!" She exclaimed.

"I don't believe you."

"Well, buddy, you had better." She stood and stomped back into the cabin. She started to crawl up the steps but stopped. Instead, she felt her way to the couch and passed out on it, still wearing what she had worn all day.

Tom looked at Olivia and said, "This has been an interesting day." He downed his last shot of vodka, took her hand, tugged at her, and said, "Let's go to bed and do the wild thing."

Olivia shrugged, "That's the best offer I've had today."

Tom smirked, and they went upstairs, fell into bed, and made passionate love. When they lay on their backs, hot and sweating, Olivia thought she heard thumps under the bed; in reality, she felt thumps that rose through the mattress.

Hidel, locked on course to pleasure himself, didn't slow his actions. Tom said, "I think I do hear something." He put a finger to his lips to indicate to Olivia to be quiet. He slowly slid off the bed and raised the bed covers to look under it. He saw a panel with painted spiderwebs, but he squinted and saw two tiny latches. Deftly, he opened them, lowered the board, and saw Hidel finish his mission. Hidel stared wide-eyed at Tom, who, in justified rage, grabbed him and pulled him from the hiding place. Anger roared through Tom as he grabbed Hidel with all his strength. Seeing a fully grown, balding man emerge from under her bed with his pants around his ankles, Olivia screamed and held the blankets up to her chest. Then she cried, "That's him. That's the man I saw the other night."

Destiny woke downstairs, nosily clambered up the steps, and stumbled into the bedroom because of Olivia's scream. She immediately saw Hidel, but she didn't know if he or the huge, fake spider scared her more.

Tom pushed Hidel, who didn't resist while attempting to pull up his pants, to a chair, wrapped his belt around him and the chair, and tried to secure him. There was no need because Hidel would not resist. Tom pointed at Olivia, "Call-call the casino security."

Hidel said nothing while they waited for security and didn't try to run. He knew they'd haul him to jail, and that's what he wanted. From the last time Jeck beat him, he desired to get away. He wanted to leave Jeck ever since they stayed at the detention center. He felt safe there.

From below, Jeck listened for any words from Hidel but didn't expect any. Hidel had never ratted on Jeck. In the past, Hidel had served some jail time for Jeck. Because they were twins and undocumented, authorities often confused Hidel for Jeck when they were separated. Hidel loved the solitary time in jail, where they fed and clothed him. He wanted to go back again. A wry smile came to Jeck's face. With Hidel in jail, Jeck hoped he'd have more time to deal with Destiny.

Before security arrived, Andre strolled into the bedroom, where Tom watched Hidel.

"Who's this?" Andre held a large glass of bourbon and leaned clumsily against the door frame. Destiny moved away from the door but not very far into the room to avoid looking at the large, fake spider hanging on the wall. Andre continued, "Oh, have you been screwing this guy too?"

All three looked at Andre in shock. Tom said, "Hey, guy, can we not do this now? Security is on the way."

Two security guards arrived, and they listened to the story. Soon they cuffed Hidel, who put up no resistance. Destiny sat on the bed, trying not to draw Andre's attention. The fear of the spider and the excessive alcohol made her want to vomit. One guard asked Tom to repeat the information about where they found Hidel. Tom said, "Under our bed," he pointed at the latches on the board he had pulled out to find Hidel. The second guard crawled to his knees and pointed a flashlight under the bed. The remaining sides under the bed looked permanent. He couldn't detect a double hidden door. Jeck hid them well. He assumed Hidel had crawled under the bed and hid until the married couple retreated to bed. By the looks of it, he assumed they had engaged in sex while the man was under them.

Embarrassed that someone had been under the bed while they had sex, Olivia's face turned crimson. She stayed quiet but stared sternly at Hidel.

The security guards explained that they would hold Hidel under lock and key in the casino until the morning.

August 7

When transferred to the county jail, Hidel didn't grapple with the police. He meekly did what they wanted. The police fingerprinted him. If the county database had been better, they would have found that he had done time in Rising Sun, Indiana, a few years back. As it was, because of his good manners and no record the authorities could find, they set a date for trial and released him. Hidel hid in a trash dumpster for the rest of the day while he thought about his next steps.

Chapter 20 August 7

Last evening's excitement and excessive drinking exasperated Destiny's EIB. While coughing and wheezing, sleep alluded her. By morning, she woke from the little sleep she had, with her mind in a fog. She wondered how she wound up on the sofa in her street clothes. Because of the EIB, her mind wasn't completely clear, but she slowly recalled the events of the night before. She coughed. Suddenly, she felt the presence of someone else. She raised her head and looked behind her.

"How long have you been there?" she asked between coughs.

Olivia stretched her arms and said, "About a half hour. How do you feel? I must say that you tossed and turned in your sleep while I sat here." She didn't mention the couple of times that Olivia heard Destiny whimper in her sleep.

"Not good."

"I'm sorry about last night."

"You didn't do anything wrong." She glanced up as if she could see Andre sleeping upstairs.

Olivia stated, "Well, maybe the time has come, and you were correct for wanting to leave Andre. I've never seen him so abusive."

"It's the drugs."

"That's no excuse."

Destiny grimaced. "Well, I can tell you one thing for sure. I'm not going gambling today." She coughed extensively. She felt too exhausted to go the breakfast. When she finished coughing, she said, "I sure can't do a day of gambling and drinking." She sat up, and Olivia moved to the couch and sat next to her.

Olivia massaged her shoulders. "I'm still here with you, and we will let the boys go do their thing."

"The boys, huh." Those words had a different ring after Andre's words and Hidel hiding under the bed last night.

"Well, you know what they say, boys...."

"I don't want to hear it right now." Destiny motioned with her hand as if to move the entire conversation away from herself. "You go on over to the casino. What I want is a hot bath by myself and a long nap. My cough, sore throat, and upset stomach kept me awake most of the night." She looked at Olivia, and her wide eyes closed in exhaustion. Olivia stared at her as one tear rolled down her cheek. Destiny said, "He didn't do anything to help me, and he went to bed and snored all night. I could hear him down here."

Olivia kissed her forehead and said, "Okay, you take care of yourself." She put a finger to her cheek, "Do you need me to run and get you anything?"

Slowly, Destiny shook her head no. "A person with EIB knows everything we need to have on hand, even when traveling."

Olivia stood, softly patted her on the head, and then proceeded up the stairs to Tom, where they prepared to leave.

Andre, not sure what happened the evening before, but seeing that his wife didn't sleep with him, figured that he should keep to himself and not interact with Destiny. Within a half hour, he slid out the front door by himself.

When Olivia and Tom came downstairs, she looked in on Destiny. "Did you see or talk to Andre?"

"Saw but didn't talk. He snuck out the door about ten minutes ago."

"Well, maybe that's for the best, so you two can have a cooling-off period."

Destiny frowned and wanted to say 'Whatever,' but she knew her friend cared so much about her. Destiny rose from the couch, coughed more, and struggled to make her way past Olivia. At the foot of the stairs, she turned, looked at Olivia, and said,

"You two go have fun. Don't worry about me. I've handled this situation before."

Olivia didn't know if she referred to the EIB or Andre. She thought about it but decided to leave and let Destiny take care of herself. She reached for Tom's hand, and they walked out the front door. Soon after they left, Destiny stripped down and slid into a hot bath. She hoped it would help with the stiffness in her chest. As she began to slide one foot into the bath water, she watched through the upstairs bathroom window and saw Olivia and Tom walk away from the cabin. Frozen for a moment, she considered that they seemed disconnected and quiet as they walked. They weren't the chatty friends she had known for years. She looked around the cabin's bathroom, where paint simulated dripping blood as if it flowed from the HVAC duct. She mumbled to herself, "This place may have been a bad bet." She smirked and said, "No pun intended, dear Dee."

She immersed her naked body in the hot bath water with that thought. The steam immediately helped open her sinuses. She closed her eyes. Exhausted, she fell asleep immediately.

Within an hour after breakfast, Tom won $5,000 on a slot machine. The noise attracted attention, and he thought some people had scoped him. It made him nervous, but he continued to play and drink. After another hour, when he poured $400 of his winnings back into the machine, Tom walked to the blackjack table to check on Olivia.

"How's it going?" He asked earnestly. He put a hand on her back and massaged her because he knew the action the night before left her tense and lost in thought. Mostly, she thought, *How can something like that happen? What a creep.*

She glanced at Tom and said, "You know me. Steady as she goes. I bet the small bets where I win little but lose little."

Tom said, "Let's go to the bar and travel to Paris and Rome and back. He referred to a drink that consisted of prosecco, Marie Brizard peach, and peach bitters. They sipped their bubbly drinks with strong citrus and a lingering vanilla taste.

Olivia said, "They made this perfectly. This was a great suggestion." She looked Tom in the eyes, put her hand on his, and earnestly asked, "How are you?" From his smile, she could tell he had won a lot that morning. "Wow, big winner today and my knight in shining armor last night."

Tom leaned his head to the side. "Just doin' what a guy has gotta do." He didn't like it when people bragged about him.

They sat silently for a moment, and then in unison, they exclaimed, "How did he get under our bed?"

Tom added, "And more importantly, how long had he been under there?"

Olivia shivered at the thought. "The creep."

"Yes, he was a creep, but did you see the sadness on his face, especially in his eyes? When I grabbed and pulled him out, it was," Tom tried to imagine the image he saw under the bed. "It was as if he wanted me to take him away."

"I don't know. It's sad and creepy." She sipped her drink and added, "I'm glad we got him out of there before Destiny stayed alone today. Poor girl. Andre's drug-induced state has them on edge."

"Well, you certainly can't tell it by Andre's reactions." Tom stood and glanced at the poker table.

Olivia said, "Oh, he's just out of it with the medication. He'll come around."

"I don't know. Andre accused her of some awful things you and I know aren't true." Tom and Olivia had chosen to sit at an outer counter away from the bar. They sat next to a fake picket fence that divided the casino and bar.

Edgy, both Tom and Olivia jumped when a man spoke. "Hey, nice going, big fella. We saw that you won big this morning." She watched two strangers walk closer to them.

Tom sized up the two men. He put a hand on the chips on the table. His look of concern immediately informed the two men that Tom thought they were poised to steal from him. The second man said, "Whoa, whoa. It's not what you are thinking.

We are here to offer a little reward at a small cost. You know. High for you and cash for us." The man reached for something in his pocket, which scared Olivia. On the other hand, Tom smiled and patted the man on the shoulder.

He said, "Not this time. Not any time in the future. Good luck to you, but I'm not buying."

The first man asked, "Sure?"

"I've never been so sure in my life. Now I'm going back to the conversation with my wife."

"Well, congratulations on a beautiful win and a beautiful wife." The man looked Tom in the eyes, "Well, if you change your mind...."

"I won't. No hard feelings, all right?"

"No hard feelings." The two men looked around the room and quietly walked away.

Tom turned his attention to Olivia. "That's two sets of drug pushers in a few days. I had no idea the drug culture permeated this place."

Olivia said, "Well, it is southern Indiana."

Tom mused. "The opportunity will always be there. The desire will always be here." He put his hand over his heart. "But as long as I'm in love with you, I'll always say 'no.'"

Chapter 21 August 7

Destiny lay almost comatose in the hot, soothing bathwater because she was tired, sick, and in anguish. She woke with a start. Only for a second, she felt someone reach from behind and place hands and a cloth over her mouth and nose. She kicked at the water and struggled to free herself from the stranger's hands, but he was too strong. Soon she passed out, not recognizing the smell of dimethoxymethane. Jeck reached into the water and pulled the plug to drain the water so as not to leave a clue that she had left the bath unexpectedly.

Jeck pulled her still form out of the bathtub, picked her up, and carried her with arms drooping toward the floor. The excitement of capturing such a beauty almost overwhelmed him. Soon he restrained her on his hand-made torture table in the basement. As he did with the old man, he contemplated what to do with her. While she lay, passed out, he bent down with his nose an inch from her lips. Moving down, he sniffed her breasts. He smiled. They smelled just like the bra Hidel had stolen. "The bra!" He exclaimed out loud. Rubbing his hands together, he retreated to his dresser, where the bra hung on one of the drawer knobs. He returned to Destiny, fascinated with the view of the beautiful, naked woman on the table. He'd watched her skinny dip but never saw her this close. "Such beauty, Andre, and you waste time gambling when you could be with her." He approached the table and put a hand on her bare feet. He slid his hand along a leg and torso. The feel of her smooth skin excited him like no other sensation he'd ever felt. As he moved upward, he raised an eyebrow when he saw her shaved pubic area. Naively, he said, "Hum, just like the little girl in the hippie commune."

When he reached her breasts, he placed the pink bra on her, but the see-through lace didn't tighten on her breasts. With both hands, he pulled the bra hooks around her body while he lifted her shoulders and hooked the bra into place. He stepped back and muttered, "Much better."

Destiny began to wake. Her eyes fogged over from the effect of the DME. Slowly her vision cleared, and she screamed. She thought she saw Hidel's face just inches away from her breasts. Adrenaline overcame her EIB. Fear made her entire body tingle like one-hundred needles poked into her skin. She felt the same prickling sensation with heat on her face - as if it would explode. She screamed again.

Jeck jumped up and down and clapped. "Scream! Scream all you want. No one will hear you." When building the soundproof basement, Jeck and Hidel checked to see if they were successful. They took turns screaming from the basement while the other one climbed the stairs to the main floor and listened. Neither heard the other's screams. Even though Destiny continued to scream, she began to assess her situation. Bound to a table resembling their cabin's torture table, she furrowed her eyebrows and began to look around. "Where am I?" She imagined he moved her out of the cabin while naked.

"You are with me. Oh, I know what you are thinking! Let me clarify something for you. I'm not Hidel, whom you folks captured last night. He and I are identical twins." Then he stood straight and grasped her hand below the binding around her arm. He introduced himself, "I am Jeck. I worship the day you were born."

Destiny dug her thumbnail into his hand. Jeck turned red with rage and pulled his hand away, which caused her fingernail to tear at his skin. He pulled an arm up as if to backhand her, but he stopped himself. "No, no, no. That won't do. I don't want to harm you. I want to make love to you. Time will bring you around. You will see." Jeck turned and walked away. He decided to visit the others in the casino. At the door, he turned and looked back at Destiny. Staring only at her naked body, he reached for the light switch and turned the lights off. "I don't think you will enjoy pitch black when I leave and close this door.

Think about it while I'm gone. If you don't like it, you'd better be nice to me. We will work out a compromise."

He stopped at his basement kitchen and picked up a fish oil capsule. He entered the cabin's main floor through the secret door, walked into the couples' kitchen, and poured Andre's vodka down the sink. He poured the wheat vodka into the empty bottle and added all the fish oil from the capsule. He shook the bottle, set it down, left the cabin, and walked to the casino.

Jeck carefully stayed far enough away from Andre and the others as he watched. The delight of holding Destiny captive while he observed Andre thrilled him with excitement and a feeling of power he had never experienced. While Tom and Olivia drank conservatively, Andre gulped down bourbon. Jeck patiently waited and followed them back to the cabin when they resigned from gambling for the day. He lagged behind them until he reached the briarwood, where he hurried to the back of the shack and returned to the basement. When he flipped on the light, Destiny twitched, tugged at her bindings, and screamed. Jeck put his hand to his face, walked up to her, and said, "For your information, your screaming will not help you. In fact, you will miss out on what they say." Jeck pointed with his eyes toward a large screen on the wall while he flipped a switch on the projector. Immediately, Destiny saw Andre, Tom, and Olivia moving about the cabin's main floor. Andre walked to the refrigerator and grabbed a beer. He hadn't weaned off the medicine, so his giddiness and delirium continued.

Tom and Andre's friendship developed because of Destiny and Olivia's friendship. Tom never considered him a close friend, and Andre had certainly tested that relationship with his crass behavior toward Destiny. She insisted that the drugs were responsible, but Tom knew the combination of drugs, attitude, and alcohol posed a real threat. Still, he avoided confronting Andre and decided not to interfere. Instead, Tom climbed the stairs to go to his bathroom, and Olivia followed, but at the top of the stairs, she veered off to locate Destiny. When she entered that bedroom, Jeck flipped the monitor, and he and Destiny watched Olivia.

"She's not up here," Olivia told Tom and Andre. "Where could she be?" Olivia stepped into the bathroom. "She's not in here." While Olivia searched, Destiny watched the monitor and became quiet as tears rolled down her face. She listened as Jeck switched monitors from room to room until the watched Tom pee. Destiny turned her head to avoid watching, but Jeck grabbed her head and made her watch the monitor. Tom came out of the bathroom and said, "I'll go outside and look for her."

Andre walked to the dining-room table and gulped down a beer while he poured a neat bourbon. Already drunk, he proceeded to get sloshed as he mourned his gambling losses. Destiny saw him, not knowing what he thought but disturbed that he wasn't looking for her.

Jeck turned on the outside monitor, and they watched Tom search. Destiny squinted her eyes in sad wonderment at how much Jeck had watched everything they had done for the past week. Moments later, Tom and Olivia returned to the table where Andre sat. They joined him, but not in drink.

"She's not outback. There's nothing on the beach like she might have gone swimming."

Olivia said, "The car is still here, so she didn't leave in it. If she had decided to join us at the casino, she would have found one of us and let us know. We didn't cross paths on the way back here."

Andre smirked. "I'll tell you where she ishh." He slurred in drunken disarray. "She's whoring with that jerk that bought her a drink."

Destiny sobbed so hard the restraints bruised her arms when her body shook. Jeck patted her on the shoulder and said, "Now. Now. It's best you learned the truth about your betrothed." This pleased Jeck, but Destiny sobbed harder, at times, gasping for air.

Olivia slapped Andre. "You are drunk. Your wife is missing, and you make an absurd accusation." She turned to the phone, picked it up, and called the casino security. Tom listened to what Olivia reported while Andre passed out. His head thumped on the table, barely missing his glass of bourbon.

The casino operator connected Olivia to security. She said, "This is Olivia Martin. I want to report a missing person." Tom only heard silence, then Olivia answered, "Yes, this is the cabin where you arrested that hideous man last night." Tom watched Olivia's jaw drop when the security guard said, "This is a casino. People do weird things. Your friend will probably return late tonight or tomorrow morning." She hung up the phone.

Olivia marched straight to the refrigerator and pulled out the bottle of vodka. She plopped into a chair at the torture table and took a big gulp. Her eyebrows dropped, her nose wrinkled, and she blew a raspberry. "That shit's disgusting. Why does it taste fishy." Without thinking, she sat the bottle between Andre and herself. Then she saw Tom's surprised expression.

Pointing to Andre, Tom said, "He certainly doesn't need anymore." Tom pulled the vodka away from Andre.

Olivia sat contemplating her next move. "I'm going back to the casino. You stay here in case she returns." Olivia glanced at Tom and the vodka. She grabbed the vodka, gulped another slug, shook her head in disgust, and handed the bottle back to Tom.

Destiny stared at the monitor, where she watched and heard Andre snore.

Chapter 22 August 7

They didn't find Destiny. Tom attempted to wake Andre but failed. In a hopeless state, they retreated to bed, where they slept restlessly.

August 8

Before sunrise, Andre woke and inspected the bottle of bourbon and vodka. He reached for the vodka but then hesitated. He grabbed the bottle of bourbon, took it upstairs to bed, and said, "I might as well go with what brought me here."

That morning, Tom and Olivia sat at the table, sipped tea, and waited for Andre to wake up. Tom had inspected the couple's bedroom. He saw Andre lying face down and the bottle of bourbon lying empty on the floor. As he had figured, Destiny wasn't there. When Tom entered the kitchen, Olivia asked, "How can this happen? Andre fell apart since the crack on the head, and Destiny is missing." She cried into her hands. She jumped when the doorbell rang. The crumbling situation of their vacation and the loud doorbell chime that sounded like a passing train whistle almost caused her to piss her pants.

Tom jumped up to answer the door before the visitor pressed the button again. Too late, the obnoxious whistle whooshed through the cottage again after he opened the door. A casino security guard jumped back at the sound. He shook and said, "I'll never get accustomed to that irritating doorbell."

"Especially with a hangover," Tom said, rubbing his temple. "You are the first person to use the doorbell since we've been here. We'll have to ask management to turn that down." He rubbed his head and asked, "What can I help you with?"

"I'm Jim Castin, captain of the security crew here at the casino. I'm following up on the reported missing person call that Olivia Martin placed last night." He glanced up from looking at a printout. "Has the missing person returned?"

"Not that we know. We've looked all over this morning."

The man tapped his pen on the notepad. "Humm. They usually show up the next morning while staying at the casino." He didn't say but implied the lost person shacked up with someone for an evening.

Olivia joined them at the door and said, "Destiny isn't like that."

"Okay, can I come in? I've got a few questions."

"Sure," Tom led him to the torture table.

The guard shook his head and said, "I'll never understand why the owners picked this macabre theme." He looked at the couple and said, "Or why people book it." He hesitated, waved a hand at them, and said, "No offense."

Tom said, "None taken. We booked it on a whim, which I think we regret now."

Olivia headed to the kitchen and asked, "Would you like some tea?"

"That would be nice. It was a late night for me too. Okay, I got on the security guard's case about not taking this seriously when you called last night. He is new, but I assure you that the casino is taking this seriously because of the previous incident. So, do you mind if I ask some questions?"

"Fire away."

"Is her significant other here?" He held his hand up and acted as if he put quotes around the words, significant other.

"He's upstairs sleeping off a hangover. You may know that a branch fell on his head the other day. We took him to the infirmary." Tom shrugged and said, "Well, he's been on the prescription drug they gave him and drinking alcohol."

"Any chance, he...."

"Let me stop you right there. He would never harm Destiny that way."

"Okay, can you describe Destiny?"

Tom looked at Olivia, who brought tea for Jim and refreshed Tom's and her drinks. She knew that Tom didn't want to describe their beautiful friend. She said, "She's tall, about five nine with a terrific figure. What stands out about her is her big, piercing, coal-black eyes and skin. Her hair is long and straight."

"Do you know what vehicle she's driving?"

"The only vehicle we arrived in is my Charger sitting in the driveway. If Destiny drove away, it was in someone else's car."

"Do you know if she's had any interaction with anyone since she's been here?"

"Well, there was the creep we called you guys about, and you took him away. He had been staring at her for days."

"Yeah, about that, he was released from the county jail this morning pending a court date."

Tom shook his head in disgust at the legal system. "How could they?"

Andre walked into the kitchen, grabbed a cup of coffee, and joined the others. He recognized the security guard's uniform and asked, "What's the latest?"

Olivia said, "We are trying to find your wife!"

"I told you yesterday; she's probably shacked up with that guy who bought her the drink."

Tom winched, "What's wrong with you? You know Destiny wouldn't do that."

Andre rubbed the back of his neck. "There's plenty of surprises in this relationship."

Jim injected himself into the discussion. "Can you help us determine when and where to look for this man on security video? Do you think you can identify him?"

"Sure. I played poker with him. I've got a great memory for faces. If you'll excuse me, I'll go upstairs and clean up. I assume I can come into your office to identify him on your security video after I clean up."

Jim nodded affirmatively.

Andre walked through the kitchen, grabbed the bottle of vodka, and proceeded upstairs.

In the basement, Jeck played the audio and video from the four talking on the main floor. He said, "They know about me. That will make me famous."

Destiny admonished, "They'll think it was Hidel. Don't forget they don't know you're twins."

Jeck acknowledged her point as if they were having a civil conversation.

Her bladder was about to burst. She'd asked several times to go to the bathroom, but Jeck wouldn't let her move. Destiny couldn't hold back anymore; she urinated while strapped to the table. Jeck jumped up and down again and clapped. "I was waiting for that to happen." He ran to the kitchen closet, pulled out cleaning supplies, and started to wipe up the mess. Occasionally, he sniffed the towel. "Now lift your bum so I can clean under you." Destiny burst into tears again and lifted her bottom only slightly because of the constraints.

Upstairs, the security guard continued. "Is anything else missing."

"Like what?"

"Anything. Clothes, trinkets."

"We never thought to look for that." Olivia stood, but before she moved any farther, she said, "Well, a bra went missing a couple of days ago."

"Before or after we arrested Hidel?"

"Before."

"Well, he was in the house. That might explain that."

Tom looked at Olivia. He resisted saying, 'I told you I didn't take it.' Olivia knew what he thought even without the words and patted him on the shoulder.

She mouthed, "I'm sorry." She ran up the stairs to rifle through Destiny's drawers. She heard the shower running and hesitated at the door. She had seen Andre naked, but she didn't open the door. She assumed Destiny wouldn't have left anything but toiletries in the shower room. Satisfied, she returned downstairs. The guard sipped on his tea when she returned.

Olivia said, "Everything is there except that bra. That's odd. It's as if she left the house nude."

Below them, Destiny screamed and cried while Jeck perched himself on the torture table with his knees between her legs. He pried them apart. Destiny nearly passed out from the shock. She hung onto consciousness until she saw someone move silently behind Jeck. She immediately recognized Hidel. Jeck began to follow her gaze. He didn't see Hidel raise a crowbar and swing it firmly down upon the back of Jeck's head. Jeck's facial expression froze in shock in front of Destiny. Quickly, Hidel pulled the crowbar back and delivered the fatal blow. Slowly, Jeck's body tilted across Destiny's leg before he fell onto the floor.

Destiny raised her hands as much as possible to get Hidel to unbind her. Instead, he ran to his bedroom, came out with a blanket, and covered Destiny. Then, he loosened the bindings on her arms. She immediately sat up and took the bindings off her legs. When she sat up, the blanket slipped and revealed her breasts in the see-through pink bra. Hidel turned his eyes. While he would have gazed if she swam naked, he couldn't bear to look because his brother had kidnapped her. Destiny stood up and wrapped the blanket tightly around the length of her body.

Close to the same time Jeck died, Andre took his last sip cf the tainted vodka. He fell dead upon the shower floor. Even after his death, Jeck exerted one last blow to Andre.

Chapter 23 August 8

What Hidel did next surprised Destiny. He apologized to her, then walked over and flipped a switch that opened the hidden door between the downstairs apartment and the main floor.

Tom jumped when the door opened. The wall behind the fake door slid to one side. It looked as if the wall moved on its own. All three who had been sitting at the table approached the opening. They heard Destiny say, "It's okay; you can come down."

Olivia shoved Tom aside and ran down the stairs. She wrapped her arms around her best friend. "We've missed you so much."

By that point, Tom and the security guard found Jeck's body on the other side of the table. The guard reached for and unholstered his gun and pointed it at Hidel while pointing a finger at Jeck's body. He asked, "Did you do this?"

Without a word, Hidel affirmed with a nod of his head. Then he pointed to the cold storage room door. The guard kept his eyes on Hidel and carefully stepped to the door. Hidel put his hands up and walked past the guard. When he reached the cold storage door, he opened it. Everyone but Hidel winced at the stench of the old man's dead body. The putrescine smell made Olivia want to puke. Oddly, Tom noticed that putrid smell but also detected a second smell. "Why do I smell cheap perfume?"

The security guard, who had previous experience with cadavers, nodded at Tom. He was assessing the stage of deterioration. "That's the result of some bacteria on the man when he died." He covered his nose but inspected the man more closely. After a moment, he said, "I'd say this man has been dead less than a week."

The guard handed the gun to Tom and said, "Hold this." He then proceeded to handcuff Hidel, who didn't resist. "Two murders. You are going away for a long time."

Destiny protested while she pointed at Jeck. "But this was self-defense. T-this one kidnapped me and was going to rape me when Hidel hit him with a crowbar."

The guard looked around the once-hidden room, "He's still going to jail, I am sure, without bail until he stands trial." The security guard walked Hidel to the patrol car and put him in the back seat. Two security cars and one county sheriff's car pulled into the cabin's drive because Jim had called for them. Tom and Olivia watched. The guard turned toward them, held his hand out, and said, "I'll be back in an hour with the manager. In the meantime, this crew," he pointed at the three vehicles, "will

assess the crime scene and remove the bodies."

Chapter 24

Destiny didn't watch the comings and goings of the security and sheriff's vehicles. She wanted to take a shower. She immediately ran up the stairs, wrapped in the blanket Hidel had given her. She screamed when she opened the bathroom door and found Andre face down, nude, and in a pile of puke. The vodka bottle lay at his side.

"Baby, baby!" She cried as she touched Andre and turned him over. Tom and Olivia turned their attention to Destiny.

"Tom, stay with them," Olivia nodded toward the security men. "I'll check on her."

When Olivia entered the bathroom, she shouted, "Nooooo!"

Destiny sobbed as Olivia knelt to hug her. "H-h-e's dead." She reached for the vodka bottle, but Olivia touched her hand and stopped her.

"He must have choked on that. I'm not sure, but that might be evidence." Destiny peered up at Olivia, who stood. "She shouted, up here." In seconds, the county sheriff stood at the bathroom door. He rubbed his beard with one hand while he assessed the situation.

Tom stood behind him and started to enter, but the sheriff stopped him. "We don't want to contaminate a potential crime scene any more than it already has been." He reached for Olivia's hand and guided her out of the bathroom. When he reached for Destiny's hand, Olivia touched the sheriff's shoulder and pleaded, "She's his wife." The sheriff retracted his hand. He called on his mobile radio for more backup. "We need more help at the M and M cabin," he told the dispatcher.

The two security guards proceeded down the stairs, where Jim had told them they'd find two bodies.

Later, Destiny, Tom, and Olivia filed reports with the casino security and at the sheriff's office. A deputy questioned all three of them, and after several hours, he released them. After a one-hour conversation with the casino owner, who apologized profusely, they checked out of the cottage. Olivia drove toward their respective homes. Destiny said, "I don't want to stay by myself tonight or this week."

"We'll take care of you."

Within a few days, toxicology identified the fish oil in Andre's system. It matched the capsule they found in the cabin's trash basket and other capsules in the basement kitchen. They added another murder to Hidel's case. When he found out, he smirked, "One last murder and one last trick on me, Jeck."

Epilogue August 20th, 1998

Destiny returned to the Murder & Mystery cabin with Tom and Olivia. They stood and watched a construction crew board up the cabin. Destiny filed and temporarily won a court order never to have anyone stay there again. She hoped that within the year, the place would be demolished. Olivia stood with an arm around her friend, who silently sobbed at the site. When she calmed herself, she said, "I had to watch this."

October 27, 1998

Destiny sat at a bullet-proof window in the prison as she watched Hidel approach from the other side. When he sat, she picked up the telephone. He did the same.

They looked at each other silently until she said, "I must know. Did you put the fish oil in Andre's vodka?"

Hidel shook his head 'No."

"I-I believe you." She sobbed a bit, and Hidel put his hand up to the window as if he could touch her. She asked, "Did you kill the old man?"

Again, Hidel shook his head 'No."

"I'll receive a lot of money in the lawsuit. I'll do everything to free you from this place."

Hidel spoke only two words to Destiny and never spoke to her again. He said, "Please don't." He turned and walked away.

-END-

What's Next?

In 2023, Steven Cain will collaborate with his wife, Kathryn Cain, also a novelist, on an anthology of short stories and poems.

Also, in 2023 or 2024, Steven will develop the third book in a series following **Sunset Kings** and **War at Home**.
It will follow the Hoffman farm family into the fifties and sixties and feature issues from the Cold War.

Further in the future?

Steven plans to revisit Darian and Cindy from **The Accident in Larson** when they travel to and work with a secret governmental organization investigating extraterrestrials.
He is contemplating future novels that deal with modern social frustrations with working titles **Defined** and **Angered**.

For more information:

https://www.stevenacain.com/

and

https://www.kathryncain.com/